MW01119917

Lady
RENEGADES

ALSO BY RACHEL HAWKINS

Rebel Belle

Miss Mayhem

Lady RENEGADES

Rachel Hawkins

G. P. PUTNAM'S SONS

G. P. PUTNAM'S SONS
an imprint of Penguin Random House LLC
375 Hudson Street
New York, NY 10014

Copyright © 2016 by Rachel Hawkins.

G. P. Putnam's Sons is a registered trademark of Penguin Random House LLC.

Library of Congress Cataloging-in-Publication Data is available upon request.
Printed in the United States of America.
ISBN 978-0-399-25695-0

1 3 5 7 9 10 8 6 4 2

Design by Annie Ericsson.
Text set in Dante MT Std.

For Jen Besser and Ari Lewin,
my Publishing Paladins.

Prologue

Outside Jackson, Mississippi

His head hurt.

It always hurt these days and had for a long time now, long enough that David couldn't tell whether it was getting worse or whether he'd just been hurting for so long that it was starting to become unbearable.

As always on nights like these, nights when he was in pain and felt like he didn't fit in his own skin, he thought about Harper. About Pine Grove and everything he'd left behind. It had been the right thing to do, he was sure of that. Staying in Pine Grove, making Harper give up so much of her life to protect him, it only would've hurt her in the long run. Not just physically—although God knew there was a risk of that—but everything. Her whole life, spent making sure *he* was safe? No, David couldn't let her do that. So the easiest thing to do, seemed to him, was to take himself out of it altogether. Then, if someone came after him, Harper wouldn't have to deal with it.

It had seemed like such a good idea at the time.

Even Ryan and Bee, the two people who cared about Harper just as much as he did, had thought it was for the best. They helped him get away, and David had thought . . . well, he hadn't really been sure. Getting away had been the main point, and he'd just figured he would work out exactly what to do next once he was gone.

That was before the headaches—and the visions—got worse.

Before he started having the sense that he was headed somewhere. Or being pulled in a direction. Every day he got behind the wheel of his car and drove, but he couldn't say where he was going. Only that he knew to turn here or to take this exit.

It should've scared him, probably, but instead it just felt like a relief.

David sunk farther into the booth, trying to make himself eat another bite of his burger. That was the other thing: with his head pounding all the time, eating had gotten harder, and his clothes were fitting a little bit looser. He didn't have any extra weight to lose, so he was probably looking gaunt, but since he avoided his reflection in the mirror these days, he couldn't confirm how bad he must look.

"You, uh, you need something else?"

The only other person in this fast-food place was a cashier, and she'd come around from the counter a few minutes ago, sweeping up old fries and straw wrappers. She was about his age, seventeen or so, and had straight brown hair that fell to her collarbones. She didn't look like Harper that much—God knew, Harper wouldn't have been caught dead in the orange polyester uniform the girl was wearing—but her eyes were a similar shade of green, and seeing them made David's chest ache in addition to his head. So he made himself smile at the girl even though he was pretty sure it must look like a grimace.

"I'm good," he said, and for the first time realized how rusty his voice had gotten. He didn't know whether that was from how little he'd spoken to anyone over the past weeks, or whether it was from all the screaming he was doing in his sleep. Either way, he sounded raspy and unfamiliar to his own ears, and from the way the girl backed up just a little bit, he knew it must sound awful to her, too.

Or maybe she was weirded out by the sunglasses.

It was bright inside the restaurant, sure, but not bright enough for the dark lenses covering David's eyes. He wore them there all the time now. By the time he'd left Pine Grove, his eyes had become bright orbs of golden light, and in his experience, that tended to freak people out. The sunglasses didn't completely disguise the light, of course, but they made it easier for people to think that they were just seeing something reflected off the lenses. People preferred to believe the least creepy explanation for a thing.

David had figured that out, too.

The girl went back to sweeping, and David went back to eating and trying to keep visions at bay.

Once, he'd needed help to see the future. Needed guidance and the magic of his Mage and his Paladin to see things clearly. Now he couldn't seem to *stop* seeing things, and every day was a struggle to keep himself rooted in the present. And the worst part of it was, he had no idea what the visions even meant.

Weird, fragmented images came to him—things on fire, blood on the front of a yellow dress—but sometimes, he got the sense the images were coming from another time and place. There was the dream he kept having of men on horseback, plus the one of men in robes in caves, the smell of incense heavy in the air.

There were times David wondered if he wasn't having visions at all, but simply going insane. Given how violent and awful his visions had gotten, sometimes he thought insanity might be the better option.

"Um, we're about to close?"

Glancing up, David saw the cashier standing near the counter, her fingers wrapped around the broom handle. Her hair was falling in her eyes, and she was shifting her weight from one foot to the other, the soles of her sneakers squeaking against the linoleum floor. This was another thing David had learned in the past two months. People were scared of him. It was probably more than the voice or the sunglasses: People could sense that there was something wrong with him, that he was something way past normal.

"Right," he said, gathering up the remnants of his meal, squashing his fries in the paper that had wrapped around his burger. Sliding out of the booth, he grabbed his tray and walked over to the trash can, pretending not to notice the way the girl moved closer to the counter.

It had been stupid to come here. Not only had he wasted money he really didn't have on food he barely ate, but now he'd freaked the girl out, and he hated that. David wished he could say it was because he didn't like scaring people, but the truth was, he didn't like being reminded of what he was. The more time he spent alone, the weirder he felt when he had to join the public.

It felt worse now than it had before. Back in Pine Grove, he might have been an Oracle, he might have had the glowing eyes and the occasional vision, but he'd had friends, too.

He'd had Harper.

Then there was the other part. The other truth. The reason he was spending so much time alone these days, no matter how many times he told himself that he couldn't be sure what had happened those other nights . . . to those other girls.

Hands shaking, he tipped the remains of his dinner into the trash, already planning out what he would do when he got back to the motel that night. Put the few things he had back in his bag, see if there was any extra change around the vending machine, and get the heck out of—

Then the pain came on, fast and immediate, and so intense he felt like he might actually die from it, like you couldn't hurt this much and *not* die.

Blood on a yellow dress, the taste of salt on his lips. More blood? Tears?

As if from a distance, David heard the clatter of the tray hitting the ground and gritted his teeth against the sudden fire inside his brain. Out of the corner of his eye, he could see the girl moving closer. Even though he'd scared her, she was still coming to help him, concern overriding her fear.

People were better than you'd think they'd be. Another lesson from the road, and one that broke his heart now.

She was just at his elbow when the golden light shot out of his fingertips, sending her reeling back, her broom flying from her fingers to smack against the glass doors, her lips parting with both the shock of her fall and the jolt of power David had just sent her way.

"I'm sorry," he said, and his voice was his and not his at the same time. "I didn't mean to."

He said that every time.

Chapter 1

"IT'S WRONG that I'm kind of hoping someone starts to drown, isn't it?"

From her spot in the lifeguard chair next to mine, my best friend, Bee Franklin, took a sip of Diet Coke, her shoulders lifting underneath the straps of her bright red bathing suit. "It would be if I thought you really meant it," she answered, and I sighed, pushing my sunglasses back up the bridge of my nose.

It was mid-July, the weather was End of Days hot, and the large rectangle of cool turquoise water shimmering beyond my chair looked like it would feel amazing. But, if I were being honest, I'd have to admit that wasn't the only reason I wished someone might get into some aquatic danger.

I was bored.

Turns out, being a superhero with no one to save is something of a bummer. I was a Paladin, a kind of magically charged knight, my sworn duty to protect the Oracle. Only problem was, the Oracle was my ex (well, one of my exes) and he'd taken off nearly two months ago, leaving me with no boy, no Oracle, and a whole summer with nothing to do stretching out in front of me. I'd never really liked summer vacation. I was always happiest doing things, being involved in projects, and throwing myself into as many school activities as I could manage.

Sure, there were other things to do in the summer. I'd tried camp when I was younger, but that hadn't worked out. (I might have made a good counselor at some point, but I was *not* cut out to be a camper. Bug spray, no private showers, and outdoor "plumbing"? Yeah, no.) I'd helped my mom teach Vacation Bible School for the past few years, but that was mostly grabbing glue and glitter from the supply closet or reading the occasional picture book about Jonah and the whale. No, what I needed for this summer—the last one before high school ended—was something *meaningful,* something . . . distracting.

Hence the lifeguard gig.

Blowing my whistle, I pointed at a little towheaded boy currently dunking a towheaded girl I assumed was his sister. "No horseplay!" I called out, and, once I'd decided he looked appropriately abashed, I settled back into my chair.

It made sense, this summer job. While I was supposed to use my powers to protect the Oracle, with him absent and my powers still present, I figured I could at least put them to good use. Plus the Pine Grove Recreation Club was desperate for lifeguards this year, and once I'd passed the test (I'd actually had to fake being tired during the part where I treaded water holding a brick over my head), the job was mine, complete with red bathing suit, shiny whistle, and a tall chair where I could sit all day, scanning the pool for anyone in distress and trying not to think too much about my own problems. Like the fact that while most bad breakups went something like "He sent me a *text*," mine was "He literally ran away and nearly blew up the entire town to do it."

So, yeah, I needed a distraction, hence the lifeguard job. A solid plan, but I'd been working here for over three weeks now, and not once had I needed to dive into the pool to save anyone. Which meant that I'd basically sentenced myself to a summer sweltering to death in a tall chair with only my thoughts for company.

Well, my thoughts and Bee's.

She'd applied for a lifeguard position here, too, both to keep me company and because, thanks to a tricky spell back in the fall, she had Paladin powers, too. So really, this was the most guarded pool in the entire state of Alabama. Maybe the most guarded pool in the entire *country* . . . but no one had the decency to drown even a *little* bit.

Honestly.

Of course, spending all day with Bee had drawbacks. Were it not for Bee and Ryan, my ex-boyfriend and Bee's *current* one, David never could have escaped town in the first place. And both seemed more relieved about their lives being off the magical hook than sorry about what they'd done.

I could smell hamburgers grilling at the Snak Shak, coupled with the coconut scent of my sunblock and the sweet syrup from hundreds of melting snow cones. In other words, the scent of every summer since I was a little girl. This was what I'd wanted for months now—some normalcy. So why did I feel all restless and sad?

I jumped as a few cold drops of liquid hit my arm and glanced over to see Bee with the bright pink straw from her Diet Coke still pursed between her lips. "Ew," I said, brushing off the soda she'd sprayed at me.

"You're thinking too hard again," Bee said, setting the sweaty can in the cup holder attached to her chair. "There's, like, a little black cloud over your head, Eeyore-style."

I smiled despite myself. "There is not. I'm just, you know, focused on the pool." I nodded at the water, but Bee just shook her head.

"No, you've got your patented Harper Price Brood Face on." She leaned a little closer then, the rickety chair groaning slightly. "Anything with David?"

Our powers and whole "sacred bond" thing meant that I was supposed to feel when David was in danger. But there'd been nothing over the past weeks, not even the slightest hint that he was anything less than okay. I didn't even have the sense that he was all that far away. Usually, when we were apart, I felt this ache, almost like a phantom limb or something, and there hadn't been any of that.

But then there was another part of me that worried that my *not* sensing anything might mean he was . . .

No, I didn't want to think about that.

So I turned back to Bee and shrugged. "Nothing."

She frowned, and I bit back that impulse again, the one that wanted me to remind her that if she and Ryan hadn't helped David leave town, I'd know exactly what was going on with him.

The rest of the afternoon wore on the way they all did, slowly and with absolutely nothing of note happening (other than some little kid eating both a hot dog and three snow cones, which meant I'd had to call the janitorial people to clean up rainbow-colored vomit, ugh). The pool had fairly informal hours, opening usually around nine, and closing at "sunset." By this point in the summer, that meant sometime after eight p.m.

This evening, most people had trickled out the gates earlier, probably wanting to get home in time for supper, and for once, I didn't have to round up any stragglers in the changing rooms. Bee and I threw white terry-cloth cover-ups over our bathing suits and pulled the umbrellas off our chairs, packing them up in the storage room by the Snak Shak.

"Another successful day, guarding the heck out of lives," Bee said as we made our way to the parking lot, bags over our shoulders. We took turns driving each other to and from work, and today, Bee had played chauffeur, so it was her white Acura we headed toward, parked sensibly under a streetlight. Overhead, the sky was striped bright pink and orange, studded with the occasional dark purple cloud. It was the perfect summer evening, but I still felt like my feet were dragging on the hot asphalt.

"And another day tomorrow," I said to Bee, shifting my bag to my other shoulder. "And then another one after that, and then— lucky us!—another one after that. A pie-eating contest where the prize is more pie."

Bee paused in front of the driver's side door, her keys in her hand. Her blond hair was curling from the water and the humidity of the day, her skin much tanner than mine. "Well, that's . . . depressing."

With a sigh, I tugged at the end of my braid where it hung over my collarbone. "I'm sorry. I'm the angstiest lately, I know. I really ought to start wearing black and listening to tragic songs. Maybe start a poetry club."

That made Bee smile, but didn't erase the concern in her brown eyes. "It hasn't been easy for you lately," she observed, and I felt a really bitter comment—*When is it ever easy for me?*—leap to the tip of my tongue.

I made myself smile at Bee, opening the car door. "It's probably the sunblock seeping into my brain or something. Or overexposure to chlorine."

As I went to get in the passenger seat, I happened to glance down into my bag. Frowning, I realized I had only my towel, keys, and sunglasses, which meant that my book was still at the pool.

"Be right back," I told Bee, and then jogged back up to the pool's gates. They were still unlocked; a few of the cleaning guys were emptying trash cans, picking up litter, vacuuming the pool, all the things I was very glad were not in my job description.

There was no sign of the book by my chair, so I walked across the concrete toward my locker in the changing room. The staff didn't get special rooms or anything, but we all were given our own lockers, so it was possible that my book had fallen out in there.

I kept a bright purple lock on mine and, as I spun the dial, I was already thinking about what I'd do once I got home. Bee would go to Ryan's, and while I knew I was welcome there, I definitely did not feel like third wheeling it. I could sit in my room with my book and fully give in to this black mood, or I could maybe go out in the backyard and practice a few Paladin moves.

Or, I reasoned, yanking the lock from its slot, I could go over to my aunts' place, watch whatever bad reality-TV show they were currently obsessed with, and let them shove my face full of cake.

Yeah, that's what I'd do. I could use a little spoiling and a lot of sugar and butter.

Opening the locker door, I glanced inside, looking for the telltale orange cover of *Choosing Your Path*, smiling as I imagined what kinds of cake The Aunts might have for me.

I was still smiling when the lights went out, plunging the changing room into darkness.

Chapter 2

FOR A MOMENT, there was no sound but my own breathing and the distant *plink* from the row of sinks on the other side of the wall.

"There's someone in here!" I called, thinking one of the cleaning guys had just reached in to cut off the lights.

But there was no answer, no apologetic "Sorry about that!" The room stayed dark.

I wasn't scared, exactly, but my heart was definitely pounding. If this was some jackass's idea of a prank, boy, had they picked the *wrong* girl to scare.

Adrenaline flooded me, and I threaded my fingers through the loop of the lock still in my hand. My punches were strong enough on their own, but a little extra oomph never hurt anyone. Besides, anyone who purposely scares a girl by herself deserves a broken nose.

"I suggest you turn those lights back on," I called out, my voice loud in the silence. "Let me *also* suggest that you not let me catch you, douchebag."

There was someone in the room with me. I couldn't hear

them breathing or moving or anything, but every hair on my body was standing at attention, telling me I wasn't alone. For the first time, something close to fear rattled through me. If this was one of the college boys who cleaned the pool, he'd have already made some noise. A laugh or assurance he was "just playin'." Or at the very least, I'd smell some cheap cologne.

I slammed the locker door behind me, hoping to startle whoever was in here into making a noise that gave me a sense of where they were.

And sure enough, there it was: the littlest gasp over to my right, close to the other row of lockers. There were benches between me and that area. Lock still clutched in my hand, I started to inch my way toward the light switch by the door, keeping far away enough from the benches to avoid tripping. All I had to do was move a few feet, then I could reach out and turn the switch on, but I didn't want to run. I couldn't remember if there'd been anything on the floor when I'd come in, and I wasn't a hundred percent sure about those benches. They could be closer than I was imagining, and the last thing I wanted was to whack my shin while trying to run away. No, my best bet was to move as slowly and quietly as I could.

There was a sudden breeze as someone moved—fast—right by me, and my heart leapt up into my throat while my fingers curled tighter around the lock.

For all that I'd battled all kinds of bad guys, it surprised me enough for a startled squawk to escape my lips, and I turned, trying to figure out where the person had gone. This was more than just some jerk screwing around with a girl by herself. This was legitimately dangerous. It wasn't a David-is-in-trouble feeling, but my Paladin senses were kicking in nonetheless. Not just heart-pounding, blood-racing, normal "I may get killed" stuff, but a sensation like Pop Rocks going off in my chest.

Planting my feet firmly, I drew back the hand holding the lock. In one quick, powerful movement, I shoved out. My hand hit something bony—a shoulder, I thought—but the person didn't budge.

Even though I knew this wasn't one of the pool guys, I said, "Last chance to turn on the lights, dude."

There was no answer.

They'd retreated, I thought, moved back to get a better look, but then, just as I started to turn in the direction I thought they might have gone, there was a sudden shuffle of footsteps, and pain exploded on the side of my head, sparking lights in front of my eyes.

Stunned and in pain, I staggered back, my knee catching the edge of one of those benches after all.

Another sense of movement, and I reached out just in time to catch a foot that had been aiming for my midsection. It was small, but the shoe felt heavy, the tread thick. A boot, I thought, and one that would have forced all the breath out of my lungs had the kick landed.

Using the other person's weight for momentum, I rose to my feet, still holding her (it was a girl now, I was pretty sure) ankle and giving it a vicious wrench.

The bone didn't break, but she gave a very satisfying cry of pain. Still, that motion, twisting her ankle, weakened my grip on her boot, and she pulled away, retreating back into the darkness, breathing hard.

My head and knee ached, but I had more than just adrenaline fueling me now. My Paladin powers roared to life, filling me with something almost like giddiness. This may be scary and dangerous and all, but it meant my boring summer was over, and to be honest, the idea of taking out some of my angst on someone who *really* deserved it seemed like a solid plan.

"Who are you?" I asked, my voice a little hoarse. "I mean, other than the girl I'm about to wipe the floor with."

There was a laugh, but she sounded breathless, too. "You wish. Clearly you've never met a Paladin."

She lunged then, and I kicked, my flip-flop flying, but my foot connecting with her jaw.

"Um, I am one?" I answered, and I could hear the girl spit on the floor.

"Whatever," she scoffed, and I reached out, trying to grab her. She moved out of my grasp, but I still moved forward. "No, seriously," I told her. "Aren't you noticing how I'm kicking your butt? You think an average girl could do that?"

No answer, and I racked my brain, trying to think how there could be another Paladin. There was just supposed to be me. Well, me and Bee, but David had turned Bee into—

I grabbed for the girl again, my fingers wrapping around a thin, sweaty bicep, and I heard her draw in a shaky breath. "Wait a minute. Did David make you? A blond boy, glowing eyes, terrible dress sense. Have you seen him?"

The girl answered me, but I'm going to skip over what she

said since it was like 90 percent profanity and didn't really answer my question anyway.

David *had* to have made her. Paladins could only be created when one died, passing his or her power on to another person via this kind of creepy kiss thing. Or, if you had an extra-super-powered-up Oracle—which David was—then the Oracle could make them. David had done that back in the fall, turning a bunch of girls into jacked-up ninja debutantes, but he'd then drained that power from all of them except Bee (she'd been kidnapped before David could get to her).

It was the only thing that made sense. And if David had created this girl, then she knew where he was. Maybe he was even close. He'd *have* to be. After all, when I'd been David's Paladin, being too far away from him had physically *hurt*. So David couldn't be far.

The thought made something in my throat go tight. "Tell me!" I demanded, giving the girl a shake. My fingers were so tight around her arm, it's a wonder they weren't touching. I could practically feel bones grinding, and the girl gave a little whimper of pain.

And then, all at once, it was like the strength went out of my grip. I actually felt it go out of me, like someone had opened a drain. One moment, I was all Paladin Triumphant, and the next, I was just a regular girl, the pain in my head seeming to multiply by about a thousand.

I couldn't help but stagger a bit, and the girl in my grip must've felt it because she twisted away immediately, and then before I could so much as think, her foot was shooting out, catching me right in the thigh.

It was a good move, and one I'd used myself. Hit just the right spot, and the whole leg goes numb, knocking the person to their knees. It certainly worked on me now, and as I crumpled to the gross changing room carpet, a cold sweat broke out over my entire body.

For almost a year now, I'd had Paladin powers, and I'd started taking them for granted. I'd been in a lot of scary situations, but I'd always—*always*—known I was going to be okay. How could I not when I was basically a superhero? But being a regular girl facing someone with those powers?

The girl kicked again, and while I reached out automatically to deflect it, it was basically like a butterfly batting at a Rottweiler. My fingers glanced ineffectually off her ankle, and the kick hit me high in the chest, making me bite my tongue in agony.

Dropping to her knees, the girl grabbed my braid, yanking my head up, and I had a dizzying, sickening moment of realizing that she was going to kill me. She'd either cut my throat or snap my neck or something, but I was going to die in a matter of seconds. The last time I'd been this close to someone murdering me, I'd been able to stab him with the heel of my shoe. Tonight, I was wearing flip-flops, and one of those had gone flying off in the middle of all of this.

Still, I fought. I twisted in her grip even though the movement scraped my cheek against the carpet and made me feel like I was about three seconds away from losing a whole chunk of hair. I might not have my Paladin strength at the moment, but that didn't mean I was going out easy.

But the girl just held on tighter, her knee coming to rest painfully against my ribs as she leaned closer. "Once I'm done with you," she whispered, "your friend is next. I'll be the only one. That's what he wants."

The words barely penetrated as I thought of Bee, waiting on me out in her car. I yanked my head again, trying to get the girl to let me go, my scalp burning, my face stinging. Had David told her about *Bee*? How else could she know?

But then the last thing she'd said hit me. *That's what he wants.*

"David sent you after me?" The thought hurt almost more than the grip she had on my hair.

The girl was leaning closer now, her breath warm on my face, smelling like Juicy Fruit gum. "You didn't think he could just leave you here, right?" she asked. "Not when you're the one who wants to kill him."

My head was swimming, both with pain and confusion, and I tried to twist in her grip again. "I would never hurt him," I heard myself say, but the words sounded weak, breathless.

The girl snorted, and I grimaced as her knee dug into my back. "He said you'd say that."

I tried to roll over, but she was still holding me too tight, her powers in full force, and mine . . . gone, it seemed like, so I stayed where I was, fingers digging into the grubby carpet.

"You talked to him?" I asked, and she shifted slightly. I got the impression she was reaching for something and, while that was worrying, I wanted to keep her talking.

"That's not how it works," she said. "It's more like—"

"Like you just know," I finished for her. I understood that. It was the same way I would feel when David was in danger. Orders didn't have to be *issued*; you just knew what to do.

And now David was ordering this girl to kill me? I couldn't believe that.

Something cold pressed against my neck, and I felt like my muscles turned to water, my breath sawing in and out of my lungs so quickly I was almost wheezing.

This couldn't be how I died. Not on the floor of the changing room at the local pool, cut down when I was helpless and scared.

I was just starting to coil some kind of strength together when the girl was suddenly off me, and I realized another person had come into the changing room.

Bee.

Chapter 3

Now my fear was all for Bee, and as I heard the gasps and thunks of Bee fighting with the girl, I suddenly found the strength to move. Still weak, I crawled for the door, wanting to hit the lights, but unable to get to my feet just yet. It felt pathetic, shuffling over the carpet, my whole body aching, my throat raw, but lights would help Bee, and that's all I wanted to do right now.

I shrieked as something hit me hard in the side, and then I was flat on the ground as something fell on top of me. No, *over* me. In the dark, either Bee or the girl hadn't seen me and had backed right up onto me and tripped.

"Bee?" I cried out as I heard the sickening *thwack* of a head rapping against the lockers.

"I'm okay!" she replied, and while she sounded out of breath, she didn't sound hurt. I pushed myself to my feet and lurched for the wall.

I heard a cry of pain and whirled around. "Bee!" I called again, but she was close to me now, her voice winded.

"That was her," she said, "but I didn't touch her."

The girl cried out again, and I fumbled at the wall. What the heck was going on?

But before my fingers could hit the light switch, there was a movement off to my right, and someone shoved past me and out into the night. When I'd been fighting as a Paladin, I couldn't *stop* fighting until someone was dead. How could she have just taken off like that?

The lights flared into life, and when I turned around, Bee was standing near me, breathing hard. The terry-cloth cover-up she'd thrown on over her bathing suit was ripped at the neck, nearly hanging off one shoulder, but other than that, she looked okay.

From the way she was staring at me, I guessed I looked a lot *less* okay.

Raising one shaking hand to my head, I felt my hair. "Did she tear any out?" I asked, a sudden image of myself half scalped coming to mind.

Bee shook her head. "No. It's a mess, but I think it's all there."

Crossing the room, she took my head in her hands, looking at my face. Then her eyes dropped lower, and her lips fell open a little bit. "Oh my God, she cut you."

I thought there was a little sting on my neck, and I'd definitely felt the girl hold a knife there. But *thinking* I'd been cut and having actual confirmation of it were two different things.

Grimacing, I lifted a hand to my neck, and my fingers came away red. It was shallow, but still.

"We need to get out of here," I told her, and Bee stepped back, glancing around the changing room.

"Should we try to go after her, or—"

There was no doubt in my mind that girl was long gone, and even if we did go after her, I'm not sure how much damage we could've done. I was trembling, Bee was clearly freaked out, and that girl had a lot of advantages over us.

Namely, that her Paladin strength was apparently working just fine.

"No," I told Bee. "At least not now."

We made our way out of the locker room, the pool quiet except for the occasional sizzle of a bug against the zappers. Bee locked the gate behind us before we walked into the parking lot.

"Do we need to go to the hospital?"

Every muscle in my body ached, and breathing hurt a lot more than it should have; but hospitals meant questions, and questions meant my parents, and my parents probably meant *more* questions and possibly the police.

So I shook my head, trying not to lean so heavily on Bee as she helped me out to the car. It was dark now, but the streetlights were bright, casting big, comforting pools of illumination on the asphalt as we wound our way through the parking lot. I tried to focus on the big moths battering themselves against the bulbs and not on how shaky and scared I felt. My limbs were tingling, something close to adrenaline moving through me, and I knew I was feeling my Paladin powers seeping back in. That was good. That helped me not feel like what I'd been for a second: a terrified, helpless girl at the mercy of someone I couldn't see.

Someone who had gotten away.

Bee must have felt me shudder, because she stopped, pulling back to look at me. Her brown eyes were wide enough for me to see the whites almost all the way around her irises. "Harper—" she started, but I waved her off.

"I'm fine."

I was basically the opposite of fine, and we both knew it.

"Was she just stronger than you, or is something wrong?" she asked, and I swallowed hard. Bee's own powers seemed fine, and as much as I tried to pretend that mine hadn't faded, she'd never had to practically hold me up before.

"She just surprised me is all," I said now. "And it was like I never managed to get off the back foot, you know?"

Bee nodded, but she didn't say anything. She just moved a little faster, and soon we were at her car, Bee gingerly helping me into the passenger seat. I was able to buckle my seat belt without wincing, so that felt like a minor victory, and it gave me the courage to sit up a little straighter. The sooner I convinced Bee I was okay, the sooner I would *feel* okay. Or at least that's what I hoped.

She got into the driver's seat, her keys jangling as she started the car, and I looked over at her. "Ryan," I said. "We should go make sure he's all right, let him know what happened."

Nodding, Bee glanced in the rearview mirror. "I was thinking the same thing." Her damp hair fell over her shoulders as she shot me another look. "So that was totally another Paladin."

The pain was almost completely gone now, but I could still remember just how hard that girl had hit me, how fast she'd moved in the darkness. "She said she was, and yeah, it sure seemed she was telling the truth." Grimacing, I rubbed my scalp where she'd pulled my hair.

Pine Grove sped by, a blur of trees and flowers and little shops that were closed for the night. I fished a hand-sanitizing wipe out of my purse to clean the wound on my neck—knew those things would come in handy working at the pool, but had to admit, this was not how I'd thought I'd be using them—and then leaned my head against the window, letting the cool glass soothe my scraped cheek. I knew I'd been right to hate that gross carpet in the changing rooms.

"If she was a Paladin—" Bee said, drumming her fingers on the steering wheel.

"David made her," I finished, my head aching for a whole other reason now. "She told me so. She said . . ." I wasn't sure I wanted to finish that sentence. But no, denying a hard thing didn't make it not exist. So I took a deep breath, squared my shoulders, and said, "She said he sent her to kill me."

To her credit, Bee didn't swerve the car off the road or gasp or anything, but I did think she suddenly looked a lot paler. "Why?" was all she asked, and I leaned my head back against the seat.

"According to our new friend back there, David thinks I'll kill him."

That was the time I would have liked to have seen some shock, maybe wide eyes, but Bee just took that in, too, and I could tell she was thinking hard. It was there in that nervous drumming—something David had done, too, I remembered— and in the way she chewed at her lip.

"You said he saw that once, right? In a vision?"

I swallowed hard. "Yeah, he did. But his visions don't always come true," I reminded her. "Perils of male Oracle-dom. He sees not just what *will* happen, but what *could* happen."

"That is so annoying," Bee murmured, and I didn't disagree. David had never actually believed that vision anyway. He'd told me so, plenty of times.

But Saylor had warned me once that boy Oracles were notoriously unstable. If David had ridden into crazy town, making other Paladins and thinking I was out to hurt him, what was he capable of? He'd almost blown up Pine Grove when he left, and now he'd turned some random girl into a freaking *assassin*.

"Is there anyone we can talk to?" she finally wondered aloud, turning into Ryan's neighborhood. Like mine, it was lined with tall oak and magnolia trees, and there was a tasteful brick sign reading "Amber Ridge."

"No," I answered, watching the elegant homes slide by. "Trust me, I wish there were, but . . ."

It had been David's "aunt" Saylor who'd first explained everything about Paladins and Oracles, who had trained me how to fight and told me what was expected of me. After she'd been killed, an Ephor—one of the people who controlled the Oracle—had come to town, and he'd told me a little more. But he was gone, too, died before my eyes, and with him had gone any chance of learning more. Alexander had been the last Ephor, which meant that we were completely out of adults who might be of any help.

Of course, after David left back in May, I hadn't thought we'd need any more help. It seemed like my days of chasing danger were over. To be honest, I'd been a little relieved, even if David leaving had broken my heart.

"If he's making Paladins," I said slowly, "it's because someone is making him do it. You know David would never do this on his own. Maybe Alexander was wrong and there are more Ephors. Maybe it's Blythe! We haven't seen her since Cotillion, and there's no telling what she might be up to." True, some of the stuff Alexander said had implied that Blythe was probably dead, but whatever. I was grasping at straws right now.

Bee didn't answer right away, but I wasn't sure it was because she didn't agree. I suddenly wished she'd turn on the radio or something, anything to ease the heavy silence between us.

"Is this something you knew could happen?" she asked at last, just as we pulled into Ryan's driveway. "That David could be dangerous?"

It was right on the tip of my tongue to remind Bee that maybe I'd had more reasons to want David to stay in town besides him being my boyfriend. If she and Ryan hadn't helped him leave town, none of this would be happening. I knew they hadn't done it to hurt me; they'd thought it was for the best.

And it wasn't like I'd told them about David maybe being dangerous. I still wasn't sure *why* exactly, except that I hadn't wanted to believe it myself.

"Saylor said some things," I told her, staying vague as I unbuckled my seat belt. "Let's talk to Ryan."

If Ryan's mom was surprised to see her son's ex and his current girlfriend at the front door in bathing suit cover-ups, she didn't show it, although her eyes did drift to the cut on my jaw.

But maybe she just assumed it was a lifeguard-related injury, because she smiled and said hello before ushering us inside and calling for Ryan. Like her son, Ryan's mom had auburn hair and hazel eyes, although he got his height from his dad.

When Ryan came bounding down the stairs, taking in both me and Bee standing there, his eyebrows nearly disappeared underneath that shaggy reddish-brown hair. He was wearing a T-shirt and basketball shorts, but Ryan managed to make even sloppy clothes like those look pretty good. There was no twinge of jealousy as I looked at him—none of us had time for that kind of weirdness—but I still felt kind of wistful when he smiled at Bee. It was nice having someone smile at you like that, and while it didn't make me miss Ryan, it definitely made me miss David.

That in mind, I gave Ryan what I hoped was a significant look. "Can we talk about that project we're working on?" I asked him, and he shoved his hands in his pockets, glancing over at his mom. "Oh. Right, yeah, the . . . project."

Ryan was the youngest of three boys, his older brothers off at college, and while I'm guessing there was a time his mom would have been a little more strict about her sons having girls over, she'd become a lot more laid-back by the time she'd gotten to Ryan.

"Why don't y'all head down to the rec room," she said, waving us forward. "I'll find some snacks."

"Thanks, Mrs. Bradshaw," Bee said, tugging at the hem of her cover-up.

As Ryan's mom disappeared into the kitchen, he turned to me, eyes moving over my face. "Are you okay?" he asked in a low voice. And then he reached out like he was going to touch my neck, only to think better of it at the last second, pulling his hand back. The cut just under my jaw still stung, and I tugged on the collar of my cover-up, wishing I could hide it better.

"We have a . . . situation," I said, and Ryan looked over at Bee, who was still standing nervously in the foyer.

"Of the Paladin kind, I'm guessing?" he asked, and before I could answer, he walked down the hall, opening the door to the basement steps.

"Come on," he said, gesturing for me and Bee to follow him. "And tell me what life-threatening crap we're dealing with now."

Chapter 4

"YOU'RE SURE it's David?"

We were all sitting in the basement-turned–rec room of Ryan's house, Bee and Ryan on the couch, me leaning against the foosball table, arms folded over my chest. Like every other room occupied by Ryan or his brothers, it was covered in sports stuff. Posters of basketball players, dusty Little League trophies lining the shelves, old issues of *Sports Illustrated* lying around . . . I thought of the pink and flowery living room upstairs and suddenly understood Ryan's mom a lot better.

But now I glanced back at Ryan, running my thumb along the edge of the table. Sarcasm is never the most useful tool of communication, I know that, but I couldn't help but say, "I mean, the girl was pretty clear about it, but, hey, maybe someone else is creating magically powered superhero girls? Who can say, really?"

Ryan frowned and I think he would've taken the bait, but Bee laid a hand on his leg and shook her head.

His eyes fell to the cut on my neck, and he nodded tersely. "Right. Dumb question. Obviously it's David, but why?"

"The girl said David thinks Harper wants to kill him," Bee supplied, and Ryan turned his gaze back to her. They really looked good together, I had to admit: Ryan in his T-shirt and shorts, Bee with her damp hair caught in a loosely curling braid, the torn neck of her cover-up sliding off one tanned shoulder. Take them out of this rec room, put 'em on a boat, and they could be cover models on *Attractive Couples Weekly*.

"Why would he think that?" Ryan asked, slinging an arm around Bee's shoulders.

"There was this vision he had once," I said with a little shrug, shifting my position against the table and reaching out to flick the little plastic ball between the rows of plastic players in red and blue. "And I . . . I saw something during the Periasmos, but Alexander said that wasn't something that would happen, just what I was most afraid of."

At the mention of Alexander's name, all three of us went silent. None of us had liked him—he'd been an Ephor, one of the men who controlled the Oracle, and I'd never trusted his motives—but watching someone die in front of you is still a hard thing, and we'd done it too many times.

Clearing his throat, Ryan sat up a little on the couch and glanced between me and Bee. "So what does this mean, exactly? Why is this happening?"

I chafed my hands up and down my arms. I'd never told them about Saylor's warning, that this could happen to David, and now it seemed like I definitely needed to. So, as quickly and as calmly as I could, I told them what Saylor had told me, about male Oracles being dangerous, about Alaric going rogue and killing Paladins, and about the threat that David could be on the same path.

By the time I was done, they were both staring at me with wide eyes, Bee pale underneath her tan.

"Why didn't you tell us this before?" Ryan finally asked, his hands braced on his knees. I made myself meet his eyes.

"Because I didn't want to believe it was something that could happen," I replied, and even though he and Bee exchanged another glance, they didn't say anything.

"But," I went on, "we can't be sure that's what's happening. Alaric destroyed Paladins; he didn't create them. And David ran away to escape Paladins and Mages and all of that. Do you really think he'd get somewhere else and then just start . . . conjuring up Paladins again? And why would he send one after me even if he did? That's never how this thing worked. I was there to protect *him,* not be . . . sent on assignments."

The room was uncomfortably quiet, and I had the unsettling feeling that Bee and Ryan were communicating telepathically or something. Not that they could do that—even Ryan's magic didn't go that far—but just in the way they both looked at me, nearly identical expressions on their very different features.

"What?" I asked, raising both hands.

"It's just . . . ," Bee started. "Maybe it's not really him, just the Paladin girl. *She* could've gone rogue or something. Getting rid of the competition."

Ryan was nodding enthusiastically. "Yeah, exactly. All, you know, *there can be only one.*"

I stared at the two of them, sitting there on the plaid couch

Ryan's mom had deemed too ugly for upstairs, and took a deep breath through my nose. "Okay, I have no idea what dorky movie you're quoting, but that is not happening, so. Let's move on."

They stole another peek at each other, and I found myself wondering if Ryan and I had ever done that when Bee was talking. Probably. There had been several times she'd complained about Brandon when I'd thought, "Just break up with him already!" Surely Ryan and I had shot each other looks over that kind of thing. Or maybe we never had, and that's why he and Bee worked better as a couple than Ryan and I had. In any case, neither of them argued with me.

"Moving on," Bee said, flicking her braid behind her shoulder.

"Moving on," Ryan echoed, and then frowned a little bit. "To . . . what exactly?"

It had already been one heck of a day, and I probably could have used a long bath and an early bedtime. But I was still too keyed up from the fight, still too excited that, finally, something was happening.

"First things first," I told them, rising to my feet, "we have to find him."

"So breaking and entering is a thing we do now?" Ryan asked, as we stood in the shadows outside David's house.

"I'm going to use a key," I reminded him. "As soon as I find it." I didn't mention that until a few weeks ago, I'd had my own key to David's house. I'd gotten rid of it in a fit of delayed break-up melodrama, but could kick myself for that now.

Saylor had always left a key under one of the big baskets of ferns that sat outside the front door—ferns that I'd taken it upon myself to water this summer.

But when I lifted that surprisingly heavy wicker basket, there was nothing underneath it.

Undeterred, I tried the next one. When that came up empty, I flipped the welcome mat.

Still nothing.

"Harper, it's late," Bee said in a low voice. "We can come back in the morning, look then, and—"

"It's got to be around here somewhere," I insisted, and walked back down the porch steps to inspect the yard. We were out of flowerpots and little ceramic animals to check, and there was a part of me that just wanted to go home and follow Bee's advice.

But then there was the part of me I actually listened to.

Marching back up the porch steps, I faced Bee and Ryan, hands on my hips. "Look, if there's any kind of spell to track David, it's going to be in that house. And until we find him, we can't *stop* him or find out why rogue Paladin girls are suddenly after me and Bee."

Neither of them replied to that, so I decided to take their silence as agreement.

"Okay," I said, dusting my hands on the backs of my thighs, "we're going to have to improvise."

Bee sighed, but Ryan folded his arms, staring at me. "If by that, you mean *actually* break and enter, no way."

I didn't want to have to pull this card—okay, no, that's a lie. I'd been wanting to pull this card for a while, so I pulled it.

Hard.

"Y'all do realize this is your fault, right? That if you hadn't helped David get out of town, we wouldn't be dealing with this?"

The words were harsh, I knew, but they needed to be said, and guilt is a powerful weapon to have in your arsenal.

Ryan lowered his brows, and Bee stepped forward. "Harper, we were only trying to help you, and it's not like you were exactly forthcoming about what could happen—"

I lifted one hand. "I know. I do. But it doesn't change the fact that you lied to me, and now things are potentially more screwed up than ever. So. That said, are y'all gonna break this window with me, or not?"

They didn't answer, but then I didn't really give them a chance.

Turning back to the front door, I examined the panes of glass that bracketed it, hoping my Paladin strength wouldn't fail me now. The glass wasn't particularly thick, but I didn't have anything to wrap around my hand, so I'd have to hit hard and fast.

I did, and while I definitely felt the shock of the hit, the glass broke and my skin didn't.

Reaching into the hole I'd made, I groped for the dead bolt, so pleased with myself that I didn't hear the car pulling up to the curb. I *did,* however, hear Bee's and Ryan's frantic whispers behind me, and I turned to them, about to tell them both to hush already, when the blue and red lights flashed on.

Eff. Me.

Chapter 5

THIRTY MINUTES LATER, I was standing on David's front lawn, staring at my aunt Jewel, who had still not finished lecturing me.

"Nineteen forty-three," she said, arms folded across her chest. When I'd called, she'd been asleep, so she was wearing a pale green housecoat over peach silk pajamas. "That is the last time the police had to be called on a member of this family."

"Aunt Jewel—" I started, but she just lifted a hand to cut me off.

"Now, Harper Jane, I am not upset that the police had to be called on you. The women in this family have always followed the rules too well for my taste."

From behind me, I could hear Ryan sigh. He had wanted to call his dad, or maybe mine, what with him being a lawyer and all, but I had reminded him that A) my dad did tax law, and B) no one was as good at getting out of sticky situations as Aunt Jewel.

Also, I knew she wouldn't call my mom.

"But," Aunt Jewel continued, "what I can in *no way support* is your nearly getting arrested for trying to break into your

ex-boyfriend's house." She gave a little sniff, pushing her glasses back up her nose. "Show some pride, Harper, honestly."

That stung, and I made an outraged noise, hands on my hips. "Okay, first of all, my trying to break into David's house has nothing to do with him being my ex-boyfriend."

Aunt Jewel raised her silver eyebrows, taking in Bee and Ryan standing behind me. "Is it Oracle stuff, then?"

Now it was Bee's and Ryan's turn to make outraged noises, and I turned to them, pushing my hair away from my face. "Okay, so maybe I had some conversations with Aunt Jewel last year, but"—I pointed a finger at them—"it was after I caught the two of you making out, so really, when you think about it, that's your fault, too. I was . . . emotionally compromised."

"Great," Ryan muttered, and Aunt Jewel reached out to smack his upper arm.

"Do not take that tone! Yes, Harper told me y'all's little secret, but I've kept it, haven't I?"

Neither of them could argue with that, and Aunt Jewel turned back to me, those eyebrows still up. "What were you looking for, then?"

I'd been really honest with Aunt Jewel, but I wasn't sure I wanted to be *that* honest right now. After all, she'd worry if she knew about the attack tonight, and there was no need for that.

"I thought David might have left some books behind that I could use," I told her, and Aunt Jewel smacked *my* upper arm this time.

"Hogwash," she pronounced. "I know you, girl, and there is no way you'd risk arrest just to find some books."

Rubbing the spot on my arm, I glared at her. Okay, I *tried* to, but Aunt Jewel is a formidable lady. So it was more a quick hard stare before I went back to cowering a little bit.

"She *was* looking for books, Aunt Jewel," Bee insisted, coming to stand beside me. Like Ryan, she'd known The Aunts her whole life, too, and had basically been adopted by them. "We promise."

Aunt Jewel harrumphed at that, but looked at the three of us, standing there on David's lawn, probably looking as exhausted as we felt. It wasn't that late, but, man, had it been a night.

"All three of you are going home now," she said, and when I went to protest, she just shook her head. "No. Whatever it is, it can wait until tomorrow. You're lucky I was able to convince that police officer that you were suffering the aftereffects of a traumatic breakup, Harper Jane."

That had been the most embarrassing part of this whole thing, having to look suitably ashamed while the police officer sized me up after Aunt Jewel's explanation. I wasn't sure if cops were allowed to gossip, but the last thing I wanted was people thinking I was losing it over David leaving. I was not the kind of girl who *pined,* for heaven's sake.

"Your aunt is right, Harper," Ryan said, resting a hand on my shoulder. "We can come back tomorrow, hopefully a little more stealthily."

My skin felt too tight, my legs restless, but it wasn't tied to my Paladin senses, I didn't think. This was just my regular response to being told to wait or be patient. And besides, that girl was still out there, gunning for me. The sooner I got this worked out the better.

But I couldn't argue with Ryan, Bee, *and* Aunt Jewel, all three of whom were looking at me expectantly, clearly waiting for me to acquiesce.

So in the end, I did.

I didn't sleep well that night, which I figured was a natural side effect of having been attacked and nearly arrested. And clearly it showed on my face when I showed up downstairs the next morning, because my mom took one look at me and said she was calling the pool and telling them I was sick.

I didn't even try to argue.

While she was on the phone, Dad came in, straightening his tie.

"Hey, sweetheart," he said, ruffling my hair. Even though I'll be eighteen in a few months, my dad perpetually treats me like a third-grader.

On a morning like today, I was actually pretty okay with that.

"Rough night?" he asked, and I sighed, poking at my bowl of cereal.

"Something like that."

Dad filled his coffee mug, the one I'd painted for him at camp back when I actually *was* a third-grader. He almost always used it, even though the acrylic paint meant he had to rinse it out by hand instead of putting it in the dishwasher.

"Still nothing from David?" he asked, and I bisected a Cheerio with my spoon.

As far as my parents—and everyone else in town—knew, David had left to join his aunt Saylor in some other state, and that move meant we were done. I'd tried to make it seem like it was mutual, that neither of us wanted to do long distance, but clearly I had not succeeded.

"He's been in touch," I said vaguely. Which wasn't really a lie. I mean, that girl showing up proved he'd been thinking about me.

Dad made a noncommittal sound and took a sip of coffee just as Mom breezed back into the kitchen.

"They said Bee called in sick, too," she told me, and I sat up a little straighter on my stool.

"I wonder if there's something going around," Mom continued. She pressed a hand to my forehead, frowning. There were fine lines around her eyes, and she definitely seemed worried, but I had to admit that in the weeks since David had gone, Mom hadn't seemed nearly as stressed.

Of course she hadn't known about the Paladin thing, but I think she'd picked up on . . . something. Some Mom sense of hers had alerted her that I was going through stuff she couldn't understand, and it had clearly taken a toll.

"Maybe," I told her now. "Or we've just gotten too much sun."

I tried to sound nonchalant, but I was worried about Bee and anxious to get to my phone and call her. Was she really sick, or had that girl paid her a visit?

That thought had me on my feet, muttering something about going back to bed.

When I got to my room, the light on my cell was blinking, and I checked it, relieved to see that I had two missed calls from Bee, as well as three texts, all asking where I was.

So I wasn't the only one on edge.

I called her back, and she picked up on the first ring.

"There you are."

"Sorry," I said, sitting down on the edge of my bed, tucking my legs beneath me. "What's wrong? Anything happen last night?"

Bee blew out a long breath, and I could practically see her sitting in her own room, blond hair a mess around her head. Bee always had the worst case of bedhead.

"No, but I didn't sleep because I was so paranoid that girl might come back."

"Same," I told her on a sigh.

There was a long pause on her end of the phone, and then she said, almost tentatively, "You were right. About David, about us helping him and screwing everything up."

My fingers tightened around the phone. "You were doing what you thought was best," I said, but the words were a little rote—I'd said them before, after all—and she knew it.

"Still," she said. "Ryan and I . . . Look, Harper, whatever you need us to do, we'll do it."

I glanced at the clock. It was just a little past nine a.m., but I was hoping that would mean most everyone in David's neighborhood was at work already.

"Then meet me back at David's in an hour."

Chapter 6

"Remind me again what we're actually looking for," Bee said. She sat cross-legged on the floor of David's room, her braid brushing the pages of the book she held in her lap.

Sighing, I picked a book out of the stack in front of me. The title on the spine was barely legible, the gold leaf all but rubbed away from hundreds of hands over dozens of years, but since none of the other books seemed like what I was looking for—they all seemed too new—I figured I was better off starting with that one. We'd been here for nearly an hour already, and nothing was jumping out at me. Luckily, I'd been right about the neighborhood being fairly deserted, and we'd slipped in with no trouble—no one had bothered covering up the hole I'd made by the door—but I didn't want to press my luck.

"Anything that looks like a locating spell, or something that mentions finding an Oracle. How to track one."

"Oracle GPS," Ryan muttered to himself, and I gave him a little smile.

"Something like that."

David's bedroom was dim, and even though he'd only been

gone for a few weeks, it was already starting to have that musty, unused smell of locked-up rooms. Other than the books, everything was mostly in order, the bed made up, the desk clear, and looking at all of it, I could almost believe David would be back any minute now. He'd hardly taken anything with him, and I wondered for about the millionth time how he was getting by. Saylor had had plenty of money, but I wasn't sure how David could've gotten his hands on any of it. Plus he wouldn't be able to get motel rooms. Was he sleeping in his car, or camping out in the woods somewhere?

Dire as everything was, that idea made me smile. David Stark, camping? I'd pay good money to see that. We'd taken a field trip to the nearby Boy Scout campgrounds in the sixth grade, and when they'd asked us to put up a tent, David had been hopeless. I still had a clear memory of him as a moving lump underneath a green nylon tarp, trying to get his poles stuck in the ground.

"You okay?"

I glanced up to see Bee watching me as she closed the book in her lap. "You had a weird look on your face," she added, and I shook my head slightly, turning back to the book in front of me.

"Yeah, I'm good. Just . . . thinking."

Bee's eyes dropped a little lower, and I knew she was looking at the cut below my jaw. I touched it self-consciously. The cut had scabbed over in the night, and I was hoping that meant some of my super-healing powers were firing up again.

I kept my focus on the books in front of me for nearly an hour but was starting to lose faith. Saylor had had a ton of books on

Oracle lore, but it was mostly history and stuff. Nothing about which spells to use should your Oracle go rogue, then disappear.

"No wonder this always went to crap for them," I said, tossing aside a book in a way that would've made David scowl if he'd been here to see it. "They never have anything *useful*. And the prophecies are like that, too. 'Oooh, when the black swan squawks at midnight, the stone will roll away.'"

Ryan blinked at me. "Whoa, did David ever say something like that?"

Rolling my eyes, I stood up, dusting off the backs of my legs. "I may have been exaggerating, but only slightly."

"I remember," Ryan said. "That night at the golf course, what was it he said to you? Something about choosing?"

I ignored that, pretending to be absorbed in scanning the bookshelves again. That word—"choose"—was a constant thrumming in my head. Over and over again, it seemed like people were telling me that's what I'd have to do when it came to David. I thought in the end, I *had* chosen him, but it was pretty clear he hadn't chosen *me*.

And now he was sending people after me.

"Still don't really get what the point of having an Oracle is if he can't give prophecies that make any sense," Ryan commented.

"Well, yeah," I replied, my fingers trailing over the spines of the books. "That was kind of the whole issue. The Ephors didn't just want to kill David because male Oracles go crazy—they also suck at having visions. The male Oracles don't see what *will* happen, just everything that *might* happen."

I pulled a book from the shelf, upsetting a little Lord of the

Rings figure that had been propped on top of it. There was an uncomfortable silence for a long moment, and then Bee cleared her throat. "I thought his visions had always been pretty clear."

"They were," I told her. "Once Blythe did the spell on him, it seemed like things were coming in clearer."

"Seemed?" Ryan asked, glancing over. His auburn hair had gotten longer over the summer and was falling over his forehead. "He didn't tell you?"

Ah yes, another embarrassing part of my whole Paladin experience. I'd been dating the Oracle, but he'd never really told me the truth about the things he'd see in his visions. Maybe they scared him.

Now I just shrugged at Ryan. "My job was to keep him safe, not interpret his visions," I said, and Ryan's eyes widened a little bit.

"I wasn't talking about Paladin you," he clarified. "I meant, like, girlfriend you."

And that had always been the issue, hadn't it? I'd never known which person to be, and being both at the same time never really worked.

"Maybe David needed some kind of interpreter," Bee suggested, getting back on the subject of David's prophecies, which I appreciated. "Or a—oh!" Her finger came down on one page with a thump. "This . . . might be something."

"What is it?" I asked, and she looked up at me, her brown eyes bright.

"It's kind of a mess," she said. "Like, some of it is in English, some of it in Greek, I think, but I see the word 'summoning.'"

I crossed the room to look down at the page she was pointing to. It's true, the words were a jumble, which was something I'd seen in a lot of the books Saylor had collected. Like someone had attempted a translation, but in a kind of half-baked way either because some things just couldn't be translated, or because the person had been in a hurry, copying things off scrolls or whatever. But this one also had an illustration with two guys in robes standing on a cliff top, a small pile of random things—what looked like a robe, a clay bowl, and what I was pretty sure was an empty turtle shell—gathered on the ground in front of them.

"Why do they have all that stuff?" Ryan asked, leaning over Bee's shoulder and tapping the pile in front of the robed guys.

"Maybe those were things that belonged to the Oracle?" I suggested. "That would make sense if you were trying to summon one, right? Using things connected to him? Or her, I guess."

Glancing around David's room, I said, "Grab something. Anything easy to carry."

Ryan's hand came down on my wrist, not hard, but firm, definitive. "Hold up. We don't even know this is the right ritual," he said, and then nodded back at the book. "It doesn't even say 'Oracle.'"

"That we can tell," I reminded him. "One of those Greek words could be it, and, I mean, come on, Ryan. Do you have any other ideas?"

I knew he didn't, and while I'd like to say I was a little nervous about running off half-cocked like this, the truth was, I was so excited that it might actually work that I didn't have time to feel nervous or like this was a bad idea.

Maybe I should have.

Chapter 7

WE'D DONE these kinds of rituals before, and they had almost always ended in total disaster. The last time we'd tried one, David had had a major Oracle freak-out that included his eyes going golden and his powers opening up cracks in the ground at the local golf course. So, yeah, we didn't have the best track record with this kind of thing, but that wasn't going to stop us this time.

Although we had learned to go farther out of town now.

We'd waited until night—this seemed like the kind of thing that worked best by moonlight—and picked a weed-choked field not too far past the city limits, and we'd picked it for a good reason. This is where the last Ephor, Alexander, had chosen to have his "headquarters," a fancy house that, it turned out, he'd created solely with magic. The house had vanished when his powers failed, and Alexander died not too far from the spot where we all stood now. I'm not going to lie, being back here gave me a major case of the heebie-jeebies; but to my way of thinking, it made sense to attempt hard-core magic in a place where there had once been a lot of . . . well, hard-core magic. Bee and Ryan were both less than certain about all of it if the looks they kept trading were anything to go by.

I choked back irritation at that. Okay, maybe I didn't always have the greatest plans, but what was the harm in trying to stack the deck a little? Still, my eyes kept drifting to that spot where I'd watched Alexander's eyes go blank, and I had to work hard not to shiver even in the sticky heat of the night. Also, I couldn't shake the feeling that all of this was a little . . . desperate. Like Aunt Jewel had said: Most girls have to be talked out of texting an ex, and here I was using freaking *magic* to summon back a dude who had, for all intents and purposes, dumped me.

I thrust my shoulders back and took a deep breath. "So," I said, holding the page I'd torn out of the book, "we all have items of David's, right?"

Ryan lifted the journal he'd taken from David's desk, while Bee waggled the pen. I took the jump drive out of my pocket, and we each threw our item onto the ground in front of us. In the distance I could hear a car go by, and overhead the moon was bright.

"All right, now we all need to picture David in our minds, as clearly as we can."

Sighing, Ryan closed his eyes and shifted his weight. "I'm all for finding the guy," he said, lifting one foot to scratch the opposite ankle with his toe, "if that's what you really want, Harper, but I have to admit, standing in a field on a moonlit night picturing his face feels kinda weird."

Bee gave a little snort of laughter that she tried to cover with her hand, and I frowned at both of them. "Y'all. Focus."

When the three of us linked hands, I could feel the vague thrum of magic surging through us. It wasn't strong, the way it was when we did it with David, but it was still *there*, and I took some comfort in that. So my powers were fading, or kind of on the fritz. At least they weren't gone.

But if your powers are fading, some evil voice in the back of my mind whispered, *why are Bee's and Ryan's just as strong as ever?*

That wasn't something I wanted to think about too hard, so I lowered my head, trying to ignore the dull ache still at the base of my scalp from where that girl had pulled my hair.

David. I was focusing on David. I called him up in my mind as best as I could, trying not to remember how he'd looked those last few days—his skin grayish, his cheekbones too prominent, his eyes haunted—but how he used to look, back when we first fell into this thing.

That David grinned at me in my mind's eye, his blond hair sticking up in weird little tufts, his eyes blue behind his glasses. I thought of the freckles across the bridge of his nose, and the way he would lift just one corner of his mouth in a smile. I thought of the way he called me Pres, and how his hands would flex on my waist when we kissed.

I thought of the night we'd gone out to the golf course to try to help David have a vision.

Or, more accurately, I thought of what had happened after, when we'd gone back to David's house.

Thank goodness it was dark because I'm pretty sure my face flamed red at that memory. And thank goodness Bee and Ryan couldn't read my mind during this little hand-holding sesh because, man, would *that* have been awkward.

Well, more awkward than it already was, doing a spell to literally force him to come back to me.

I don't know what I was expecting to happen. For the three of us to suddenly get some picture of where David was? Like a hologram in those stupid sci-fi movies he liked? Or that we'd just suddenly *know* where he was, the way I knew how to get to Ryan's house or how to maneuver my way to Bee's locker?

But in the end, we just stood in that hot field, grass tickling our calves, our palms sweaty against one another's, and there was no sign of David, no sudden realization of where he'd been hiding or what he was doing.

Why he was making Paladins.

Frustrated, I dropped Bee's and Ryan's hands, wiping my palms on the back of my shorts. "Anything?" I asked, wondering if they'd felt something different. Maybe it was just *me* who couldn't find David. But they both shook their heads, too, Ryan toeing at the dirt, Bee worrying the end of her braid in her fingertips.

"We could try something else?" I wasn't exactly crazy about the idea of staying in this field. I was pretty sure I'd heard something scuttle through the tall grass on the side of the bare spot where we stood, but I wasn't ready to give up. "That was just one ritual; maybe there are other things?"

I really wanted there to be, trust, but it had taken us over an hour just to find this one, and having dragged them out to the middle of a field for no apparent reason, I felt more than a little silly. Plus all the adrenaline was finally wearing off, and I was suddenly really exhausted. All I wanted was to go home, get a shower, and collapse into bed, maybe try to forget this entire night had ever happened.

But I didn't have that luxury. I might not be nearly as connected to David as I had been, but that didn't mean I could just leave him. And not only for him, but for everyone else

Sighing, I turned to head back to the car, wondering why I'd ever thought this was going to work. There had been a time when I'd prided myself on being the most competent girl in the room, the one who always knew what to do. But the deeper I got into all this Paladin stuff, the more I seemed to be screwing it up. Maybe whoever that crazy new Paladin girl had been, she was . . . better than me.

It was an unsettling thought, as was the idea that that girl was still out there.

My head full and my heart heavy, I trudged through the tall grass, Bee and Ryan following behind. We were nearly to the edge of the field when Ryan made a weird noise, almost like something had surprised him.

I whirled around. He was standing still, one hand pressed to his chest, the heel of his palm rubbing over his heart.

"What?" I asked. "Did you see something or feel something or—"

He held up his free hand, still frowning. "No. Or . . . kind of. I don't know. It was like something just . . . thumped me, but inside." He tapped his chest again.

We all stood still in the field, chins slightly lifted like we'd be able to sniff something on the wind. Which was stupid, of course, but there did seem to be a feeling in the air, a vague electric sizzle that had the hairs on my arms lifting.

Or maybe I was just hoping too hard that this had worked.

After a moment, Ryan rubbed his chest again and shook his head, his hair falling nearly over his eyes. "It's gone now. Whatever it was."

I nodded, my throat suddenly tight. "That's that, then," I said, but even as I turned to go, I wasn't sure I believed it.

But what I *did* believe is that if we couldn't summon David to us, we were going to have to find him.

I just had no idea *how*.

Chapter 8

THE COUNTRY CLUB was crowded that Sunday, which was always the case on afternoons after church. It seemed like the whole town would come out, which wasn't exactly a surprise since the Sunday buffet was pretty legendary. After last night's trauma, I could have used at least an entire plate of mac and cheese (considered a "vegetable" here in Alabama, of course, kind of the way little pear halves filled with mayo were occasionally referred to as a "salad"), and I moved through the line, happily filling my plate. I'd need another hour of training to work it off, but some things are worth the effort.

Next to me, Bee reached for the big spoon dipped into a tray of steaming green beans. "I had some seriously weird dreams last night," she confessed, ducking her head low enough so that I was the only one who could hear her.

I glanced behind us. My parents were sitting at a big round table with my aunts, and Bee's family was sitting at the next table over. Ryan sat with them, which was a little weird—there had been so many Sundays when Ryan sat at our table—but no one was really looking over at me and Bee.

Moving down the line, I picked up some tongs, poking around in the giant bread basket for a cornbread muffin. "You and me both," I admitted.

In fact, I felt like I'd hardly slept, and when I'd come down for church this morning, Mom had looked at my face with a concerned frown that told me all the concealer I'd applied hadn't totally erased the effect of the night before.

I hadn't seen David in any of my dreams, but I'd definitely felt like he was close by in them. It had been the weirdest feeling, and even now, remembering, I shivered a little.

Bee looked down at me, holding her plate with both hands. "This is going to sound nuts, but I felt like . . . like maybe I was dreaming the same things he was?"

It didn't sound nuts at all. In fact, that's exactly what I'd been wondering every time I'd woken up from another dream full of smoke and blood and a feeling of panic lodged sharp as a thorn in my chest. But if they were David's dreams, did that mean they were really visions? And if they *were* visions, what of?

Of course, seeing how scary those visions were, I wasn't sure that was a question I wanted answered.

"I get that," I said, looking up at Bee. "So maybe the spell worked a little? It didn't help us find him, but it"—I opened and closed my free hand, trying to think of the word I wanted to use—"connected us to him or something."

"I thought you already were connected to him," Bee said, and I gave an uneasy shrug.

"I am, but maybe this strengthened the bond. Or maybe we just had David on the brain, and it's manifesting itself in our dreams."

Now it was Bee's turn to shrug, and she turned away from the buffet. "Maybe," she said. "But in any case, they're not dreams I want to have."

"Me, neither," I said, trailing behind her as we made our way to our tables. Our friends Abi and Amanda were sitting near the window with their parents, both of them in mint-green sundresses, Amanda's hair in a low ponytail, Abi's loose around her face, which was the only way I could tell them apart from this far away. I would've thought they'd have outgrown dressing the same around, oh, second grade or so, but I think their parents liked the matchy-matchy thing. I wiggled my fingers from under my plate at them, and they waved back.

I also saw Bee's mom and dad, and saw the way they glanced from me to Ryan, sitting at Bee's mom's left. I gave Ryan a smile I hoped conveyed the right amount of "Totally fine with this, Bee's parents!" I knew my own parents thought the switch from Ryan dating me to Ryan dating Bee was kind of awkward, and no matter how much I tried to tell them we were all totally fine with it, I didn't think they bought it. Mom's smile was definitely a little tight when I put my plate down, and as I took my seat, she leaned closer to murmur, "Everything okay?"

"I'm fine," I told her, laying my napkin in my lap. "Ryan and Bee are actually way more suited for each other than Ryan and I were. Look how she hasn't even complained about his elbows being on the table!"

Mom shot me a wry look, one hand going to the delicate strand of pearls around her neck. "So you keep saying, and I have to admit, you really do seem . . . okay with everything."

"Of course she is," Aunt May said from the other side of the table, not even bothering to lower her voice. "Our Harper isn't one for crying over spilled milk."

My aunts ate with us after church every Sunday, and today, they were all in different shades of green. Aunt May and Aunt Martha were twins, but their sister, my aunt Jewel, was almost identical to them, all three sporting silvery perms and glasses they liked to wear around their necks fastened to sparkly chains. They were pretty much my favorite people, and Aunt Jewel was especially high on my list after Friday night. It's not many people who will help talk you out of getting arrested. As I met her eye over the linen-covered table, she gave me a little wink and I smiled back. It was funny how much better you could feel just sharing a secret with a person who loved you.

Across the table, Dad smiled at me, giving a little lift of his chin that I think was supposed to signal, "Buck up, little soldier," or something similarly Dad-ish. I wasn't sure if he thought I was upset about Ryan and Bee, or if I was just making a particularly tragic face, but in either case, I appreciated it, and smiled back.

"How is work at the pool hall, Harper Jane?" my aunt May asked, and Aunt Martha jabbed her with an elbow.

"She's not working at a pool hall, May, honestly. She works at the *pool*."

Aunt May gave a little shrug as if there weren't much difference between the two, and I caught Aunt Jewel's eye.

"It's fine," I said to Aunt May. "Not as exciting as I thought it would be, but at least I'm getting fresh air and plenty of time to read."

Aunt Martha pointed at me with her fork. "Just be sure you keep your hair up. Don't want to end up like Dot Jenkins."

I had no idea who Dot Jenkins was, but Aunt Martha was clearly going to tell me something awful that had befallen the unfortunate Dot. The Aunts collected horrible stories the way some old ladies collected ceramic angels.

"It was 1956," Aunt Martha continued, confirming my suspicion. "Swimming at the pool we used to have here at the club. Caught her hair in a drain, and that was that."

"It was 1955," Aunt May said, and Aunt Jewel rolled her eyes, pushing a chunk of sweet potato around her plate.

"It was 19–Both of You Are Ridiculous," she said. "Dot Jenkins did not drown in the country club pool. She hit her head on a dock at Lake Prater and drowned *there*."

As The Aunts squabbled over just what tragic drowning had befallen Dot Jenkins, I turned my attention back to my plate, still thinking about the past couple of days, and how close I had come to being one of those stories. Heck, that was just the last in a long line of Terrible Deaths I Almost Experienced. Stabbed to death in the school bathroom, stabbed in a college office, stabbed at Cotillion . . .

Frowning, I wondered why all the bad guys I faced were so stabby. I'd definitely need to make sure my training was more focused on anti-stabby things if I—

I was suddenly aware of someone standing over my shoulder, and I nearly turned in my seat to see who it was. The Aunts were still arguing, but my dad was glancing up with polite inquiry on his face.

And then I felt it. Whoever it was behind me, they were *radiating* power.

It all happened in the space of a few heartbeats. A hand touched my shoulder, and magic flared under my skin. What kind of magic, I had no idea, but I didn't give myself time to think. Instead, I covered the hand with mine, and as I did, shot to my feet, my other hand coming across my body to grab an arm, foot hooking under ankles to bring the person down hard. I had enough time to see dark eyes go wide as the person fell, hitting the table on the way down, rattling dishes and glasses. Next to me, I heard Mom gasp and cry, *"Harper!"* I lifted my head to meet a sea of shocked faces. My mom's closest friend in the Junior League, Mrs. Andrews, had gone pale, and one of the partners at Dad's law firm, Mr. Montgomery, was mouthing what seemed to be a couple of variations of the F-word. But I couldn't have stopped myself for anything. All I could think of was that feeling of helplessness lying on the floor of the changing room Friday night.

This time, my powers didn't falter even for a second. They pulsed through my veins, strong as ever, and I might have been smiling in kind of a creepy way.

But that smile fell off my face immediately when I realized who was on the country club floor under my foot, wearing a smile of her own.

Blythe.

Chapter 9

"Holy crap," I breathed, my fingers still locked around Blythe's delicate wrist. "*You.*"

She had one hand free, which she used to wiggle her fingers at me in a little wave. "Harper."

I was breathing hard, but as the adrenaline faded, the realization that I had just handed a girl her lunch in front of a third of Pine Grove suddenly began to dawn.

Then Aunt Jewel, bless her heart, stood up and said, "Ooh, is this the girl teaching your self-defense course, Harper Jane?"

She said it so loudly that I was pretty sure people in the next town over had heard her, so it wasn't exactly the most subtle of saves.

But it was effective, especially when Bee came over and said, "Wow, when you said the final exam could happen anywhere, I didn't think you meant the country club!"

She gave a bright laugh that was as high as it was fake, but I could feel some of the tension drain out of the room, especially when I finally took my foot off Blythe's chest and offered a hand to help pull her up.

Shooting to her feet, Blythe just smiled again and, for whatever reason, decided to play along. "And you *passed!*" she said before rubbing at her chest with the tips of her fingers and grimacing slightly. "With flying, really painful colors!"

At my side, Mom still had her palm flat against her pearls, her gaze shooting between me and Blythe. Dad was also on his feet, hands deep in his pockets, watching up over the tops of his new bifocals.

"What self-defense class, Harper?"

My head was spinning, wondering both what Blythe was doing here—and if her being here had anything to do with what had happened at the pool on Friday night—and with making sure I sold this to my parents as quickly as possible.

"Just an extra little thing I picked up for the summer," I said, waving it away like it wasn't a big deal. "You know, getting ready for college and all that. Girl has to be able to defend herself."

Considering the fact that at least half the women in this room were probably concealing pistols in their pocketbooks, I didn't think anyone would argue with that. Sure enough, people started digging back into their prime rib and potatoes.

My own family was still a little nonplussed, but Aunt Jewel sat down and started eating, which went a long way with Aunt May and Aunt Martha. They took their lead from Jewel and today was no exception. After a brief pause, they gave identical shrugs and tucked back into their food.

My parents were a little less willing to let this go.

"Self-defense is important," Mom said, looking at Blythe, who, in her bright yellow dress and high ponytail, certainly didn't look all that threatening. She kind of looked like a brunette Easter Barbie, to tell the truth. But this girl had tried to cut me with a letter opener, performed terrifying magic on David, and kidnapped my best friend, all to help the Ephors either super-charge David or kill him.

I didn't underestimate her.

"But there is a time and place for displays like that," Mom continued, "and Sunday afternoon at the country club is not one of them, young ladies."

"Yes, ma'am," I said, knowing that the easiest way to get out of this was to seem as abashed as possible, no matter how much my heart was racing. What the heck was Blythe doing here?

"I apologize, too," Blythe said, flashing my parents a bright smile. "But being prepared in any location really is one of the tenets of our, um, organization."

She looked back at me. "Can we go outside and talk for a minute?" Blythe asked before flicking her eyes at my parents again. "About the, um, self-defense class?"

Looking back to my parents, I put on my most contrite expression. "May I be excused?"

Mom and Dad glanced at each other, Dad rocking back on his heels, but after a beat, Mom nodded, and said, "Fine. But don't be too long."

Ryan and Bee were already standing up next to their table, and I jerked my chin at them.

As quickly as I could, I ushered the three of them, Bee, Blythe, and Ryan, out of the dining room and down the long hall leading to the front doors. Posture is 80 percent of projecting an air of self-confidence, so I made sure my shoulders were back, chin lifted slightly as we walked outside. The country club was surrounded by thick flowering bushes, their scent almost over-powering in the July heat, and I led our little group around the side of the building and down a sloping sidewalk, close to the tennis courts where the bushes were highest so that we'd be out of sight for the most part.

As soon we'd stopped, I whirled on Blythe and dropped any pretense of civility. "What are you doing here?"

"You summoned me," Blythe said immediately, looking around at all of us, her big brown eyes wide. "With, like, a fairly powerful spell. I felt it the second you did it. Threw my stuff in the car and headed this way. Of course, I wasn't positive *who* was summoning me, but once I hit the state line, I had a pretty good idea it was you."

"Trust me," I said, still rubbing my sore elbow. I'd whacked it fairly hard on the table throwing Blythe to the ground. "No one around here did anything of the sort. The absolute last thing—"

And then I thought of the three of us in that field with David's things, the thump Ryan had felt in his chest. The spell had been a mix of Greek and English with the word "summoning," in there, and . . .

"Mother effer," I muttered. "So that spell we did to find David paged you instead?"

Blythe reached up and pulled her sunglasses down from the top of her head. "Oh my God, seriously? You were doing a ritual and didn't even know what it was for?"

That last bit was directed at Ryan, who looked distinctly

unhappy with this development. "It's not my fault," he said, shoving his hands into the pockets of his khakis. "We didn't know what we were looking for, so—"

"So you just decided to do any magic you could find, hoping it would work out?" Blythe folded her arms over her chest. "Well, that's not incredibly stupid or anything. Oh, wait, I actually meant the *opposite* of that."

"Yes, we're familiar with sarcasm," I told her. "But the fact remains that we did the best we could with a situation that you and your bosses—or boss, whatever—caused."

Blythe whipped her head around to glare at me, and the anger in her eyes was so intense, I nearly took a step back.

"They were *not* my bosses," she practically spat.

I probably should have backed down given the look in her eye, but I'm not really good at that. "Oh, sorry, it's just that you did a thing they asked you to do, which generally makes someone your boss? See, that's more of that sarcasm I identified before."

Blythe took a deep breath through her nose, the universal sign for "I am trying so hard not to murder you right now." But when she spoke, her voice was relatively calm.

"Look, it doesn't matter if you were trying to summon me or not. Point is, I'm here now, and we all want the same thing: to find the Oracle."

My pulse leapt. The attack at the pool—what if it was actually Blythe's doing? The idea that I had been right, that David would never send people to hurt me, nearly made my knees weak with relief. "Why do *you* want to find him?"

She turned to me, wiping her palms on her skirt. "Because he's gone rogue, right? Scampered right off with more magic than he knows what to do with? Seems like a potentially yikes-y thing."

"How did you know that?" Ryan asked, stepping forward a little bit, but Blythe waved a hand at him like he was a particularly annoying mosquito.

"Believe it or not, you're not the only ones connected to the Oracle," she said. "Thanks to that little ritual I did on him at your cotillion, I'm just as connected to him as his Paladin. Magic does bond people."

"You mean like the magic that you did that had him making Paladins?" I suggested, lifting my eyebrows. "The magic that, for all we know, you're doing again?"

That seemed to genuinely surprise Blythe. She stepped back just the littlest bit, lifting her chin, her dark eyes wide. "You think it's my fault that he's descending into crazy-town?"

We were still standing just outside the country club, and I knew people would be coming out soon. Bee was already looking toward the door, probably keeping an eye out for her parents. I turned back to Blythe. "You can't exactly blame us for thinking it."

She paused, considering that, and then shrugged. "Fair enough. But I promise you, this"—she looked down at the little purse dangling from her shoulder, opening it up and pulling out a folded piece of newspaper—"has nothing to do with me."

I took the paper. It was from yesterday's edition of the *Ellery News*. Ellery was a medium-sized town, big enough to have a weekend edition. Yesterday's headline was about a missing girl from Piedmont, Mississippi, who had turned up in Ellery with no memory of how she'd gotten to Alabama.

"Read it," Blythe instructed. "The last thing she remembers is meeting some guy with, and I believe I'm quoting this correctly, 'glowing eyes.'"

My heart seemed to stutter in my chest. There was no picture of the girl, and even if there had been one, I'd never actually seen who attacked me at the pool. But, reading this, it became pretty clear this was her. Her name was Annie Jameson, and she seemed . . . a lot like me, actually. From what I could gather reading the brief snippet, she was an upcoming senior at Piedmont High School, an honor student, no history of trouble . . . I still didn't understand why she'd run off, or how she could suddenly be . . . de-Paladined. None of this made any sense, and my skin felt itchy, my nerves jumping.

Piedmont wasn't very far from here.

I was still looking at the paper when Blythe turned to me and said, "So when are we leaving to go after him?"

Chapter 10

STARTLED, I LOOKED up from the piece of newsprint. "What?"

"He's making Paladins," Blythe said, tapping the paper. "It's a little bit my fault for doing that ritual on him, sure, but it's also your fault for letting him get away."

I tried very hard not to look at Ryan and Bee, but I could sense them shuffling next to me. Placing blame was pointless at this stage in the game.

"We can't," I told Blythe now, but the words were hollow. "It's not feasible."

Blythe shoved her glasses back on top of her head, blinking at me. "Are you kidding? Isn't this, like, your entire sacred duty?"

I gestured around to Bee and Ryan. "It's . . . Look, I don't know how you got here or where you came from, but it isn't easy for us to just go gallivanting around the country for a few months. We have things like responsibilities. And *parents*."

The second the words were out of my mouth, I felt kind of bad. I mean, I had no idea if Blythe had a family or not. Obviously, she had at one time, but what did they think happened to her after she ran off to be a crazy Mage?

But then I remembered that Blythe cast a spell on my boy-friend, kidnapped my best friend, and tried to kill me multiple times—once with a letter opener—and my sympathetic feelings disappeared in a big poof.

Blythe rolled her huge dark eyes. "You also have *magic*," she said. "Buttloads of it. Mostly mine since this redheaded Ken doll over here seems kinda worthless."

Ryan frowned, one hand touching the back of his head. "My hair isn't red." Glancing over at Bee, he raised his eyebrows. "It's not, right?"

She patted his leg. "It's only a little red," she assured him, and Ryan's frown deepened.

Blythe gave a little smirk before turning back to me and cross-ing one leg over the other, the heel of her bright yellow ballet flat slipping off as she propped one toe on the sidewalk. "We have to find the Oracle and put a stop to this before it gets any worse."

She was right, I knew that, but putting my trust in her was not exactly the easiest thing to do.

When I said something to that effect, she heaved a deep sigh that seemed to come up from her toes. "I get that. But how many times do I have to say this?" Tilting her head down, she fixed me with a look over her sunglasses. "I. Am. Not. Doing this. For. You." As if to punctuate the statement, she shoved her glasses back into place with one perfectly manicured finger. "This is not about saving your boyfriend or helping you all become one happy, magic-doing, future-seeing, butt-kicking threesome—*not* like that," she added when it was clear Ryan was about to protest.

"It's about me undoing the thing I did for people who never deserved my powers in the first place."

There was something cold in her tone when she said that, something so bitter about the words, I felt like I could almost taste them. I didn't know what had happened to Blythe after the Ephors took her, but whatever it was, it had clearly been bad.

"Blythe wasn't there," Bee suddenly said, and I turned to see her standing just behind me, arms folded tightly. "When I was with the Ephors, she wasn't there."

It was weird, remembering that Blythe and Bee had that in common, being held by the Ephors, and when I looked back to Blythe, a muscle twitched in her jaw.

"Yeah, let's just say they made sure I was out of sight," she said. "It wasn't until Alexander died that I was even able to get out of that place."

"How did you know he died?" I asked then, and Blythe gave another one of those eye rolls that suggested we were all wasting her time.

"I could feel it. There was a lot of magic going into keeping their headquarters running, and even more into making sure I couldn't get out. When it just went away, I knew Alexander was gone. It was the only explanation."

That made sense, I guessed, but this was all moving so fast—and I was very aware of curious eyes on us as people made their way to the parking lot—so I decided to cut to the chase.

"Okay, but why should we go with you when we already have a Mage?" I said. "*You* may not be impressed with Ryan's powers, but he's still every bit as useful to us as you would be, with the added bonus of not being insane."

Throwing her hands up in the air, Blythe made a disgusted sound. "He can come, too, for all I care. But you need me. I'm the only one who can find the spell we need to stop him."

People were starting to leave the country club now, my parents and aunts among them, and I gave them a quick little wave before gently taking Blythe's arm and leading her closer to the tennis courts. There was no way I was going to be able to fake smile at her while my parents watched.

"What kind of spell?"

Blythe shrugged out of my grip and pulled at the skirt of her yellow dress. "Why, so I can tell you, and then you and your friends can run off and screw it up? You people don't exactly have the greatest track record with magical nuance." She shook her head, making her ponytail swing. "Nuh-uh. We're either all in this together, or we're not in it at all."

"Whatever you're doing, we don't want a part of it," I told Blythe, and when I folded my arms over my chest, Ryan and Bee mimicked my pose. Blythe looked at the three of us for a beat before scoffing and putting her sunglasses on top of her shiny brown hair.

"Okay, fine. Be the Three Musketeers and solve this on your own. I mean, that's clearly worked well for you so far. We've got a Mage who has no idea how to use his powers"—a flick of her hand at Ryan—"and two Paladins who are losing theirs." She moved her hand to gesture to me and Bee, her lips pursed slightly.

"How did you know about that?" I asked without thinking, and then from beside me, I heard Bee suck in a breath.

"Wait, that's true?" Ryan asked.

I ignored him, keeping my eyes on Blythe. One corner of her mouth lifted in a smirk. "The longer you're away from the Oracle, the weaker your powers will get. It may not happen at the same rate," she added, nodding at Bee, "but it *will* happen to both of you, Harper. And that means you're going to have Paladins coming after you without being able to fight back. Do you see *now* why my idea might be the best one?"

It was. I totally saw that. Heck, I'd always wanted to go after David rather than sitting back and waiting for things to happen to me. "Proactive" was practically my middle name, but that didn't mean this would be easy.

But if we had Blythe—and Blythe's plan, whatever it was—maybe it could work?

I felt the briefest spark of hope in my chest, and then I remembered Blythe at Cotillion. The look on her face as she'd done the spell on David. The way she'd vanished with Bee. The complete and utter havoc she'd wreaked in the few days I'd known her.

I wanted to find David, and I was curious about whatever she had planned, but trusting Blythe after everything? Was I *that* desperate?

"I understand that you don't trust me," Blythe added. "I mean, *I* wouldn't trust me if I were you." She leaned closer, and I could see my own skeptical face reflected in her sunglasses. "But there are things I know that you just don't. Spells this guy"—another dismissive glance at Ryan—"hasn't even heard of."

Reaching out, Blythe tugged my purse off my shoulder. I gave a startled squawk, but she just fished out my phone and typed into my contacts.

"Now you have my number. When the three of you decide to grow up," she said, even though I was the only one she was looking at, "you can give me a call. But I'm only sticking around for a few days."

With that, she spun on her little ballet flats and headed toward the parking lot.

But then she stopped, turning around to look back at us, her hand lifted to shade her eyes. "This isn't just about you, Harper. You or your friends. Alaric destroyed an entire *town* when he turned. He killed Paladins, sure, but innocent people, too. This whole thing is so much bigger and worse than you understand."

She nodded at my phone, still in my hand. "So you think real hard about that. And then call me."

Chapter 11

"DON'T YOU HAVE anything smutty on that cart?"

I blinked at Mrs. Morrison. It was Monday morning, which meant I was helping The Aunts with their volunteer work at the local assisted-living facility, Hensley Manor. They visited at least three times a week, sometimes arranging activities for the residents, sometimes just to chat or sneak in homemade cookies. My Aunts genuinely liked helping people, but they also liked to remind themselves that while they might be old, they weren't *that* old yet. I was usually too busy to help during the school year, but during the summer I tried to commit at least one day a week to being in charge of the mobile library, which was really just a rolling cart full of paperbacks.

Paperbacks that were not smutty enough for Mrs. Morrison.

I glanced back over the rows of spines, trying to find something that had the word "savage" in the title, finally settling on a bright pink book with half-naked people on the front, and a very alarmed-looking swan in the background. "Will this work?"

Mrs. Morrison's watery blue eyes went wide and she plucked

the book from my fingers. "You're a good girl, Harper," she said, and I smiled as I stood up, pushing my cart toward the door.

"You're welcome!" I said sunnily, then headed out in the hall to continue my rounds. As soon as I was out of her sight, my smile dropped, and I had to fight back a sigh. It had been two days since we'd done the ritual in the field, and while Blythe had turned up, there was still no sign of David.

"Harper Jane, stop scowling!" Aunt May said, coming out of another room, stuffing her knitting in her bag.

I straightened up, trying to smile. "Sorry, Aunt May. Just thinking."

She gave a little sniff. "You think too much and too hard. You get that from Jewel."

I didn't think it was supposed to be a compliment, but that actually made my smile a little more genuine. There were worse things in life than being like Aunt Jewel, after all.

"I'll bear that in mind," I said to Aunt May, pushing my cart farther down the hall.

I made a couple more stops—and a mental note to pick up some more "smutty books" at the local Goodwill—but then the soft chime sounded, signaling lunch. Stowing my cart away in the break room, I went in search of Aunt Jewel. We hadn't gotten a chance to talk after everything at the country club, and while Aunt Martha and Aunt May had grilled me about it on our way to the nursing home this morning, Aunt Jewel had been silent. Which, I knew, meant she was waiting for a chance to talk to me alone.

I finally found her having her lunch outside in the little courtyard between the buildings, and even though it was hotter than Satan's armpit out there, I went to sit next to her. Wordlessly, she handed me half of her sandwich. I peeled back the wax paper and took a little sniff. Aunt Martha's famous curry chicken salad with green apples, one of my favorites.

"I was hoping to get you alone," Aunt Jewel said after I'd taken a bite. "And ask you just what in the Sam Hill all that stuff was at the country club on Sunday."

I went to answer, but she held up one hand. "Don't talk with your mouth full, and also don't bother trying to tell me it wasn't important. Girl shows up and you go all ninja on her, I figure it has something to do with everything we've been talking about."

I swallowed. "It does. That girl . . . her name is Blythe, and she's a Mage. It's a person who does magic—"

"To protect the Oracle," Aunt Jewel said with a little nod, her silver curls quivering. "I remember what you told me, Harper Jane, I don't have Old Timer's just yet."

"Alzheimer's," I murmured, but she waved that off.

"I said what I meant, and meant what I said. So she's the same thing as Ryan, then?"

Nodding, I took another bite of my sandwich. Only when I'd finished did I say, "Yes, but evil. And also crazy. And potentially dangerous."

Aunt Jewel took that in. "So why is she here, then?"

As briefly as I could, I filled Aunt Jewel in on everything that had happened. The fight at the pool, why I thought David was in danger, the ritual we'd done trying to find him, and how that had summoned Blythe right to us. Finally, I told her about Blythe's plan to find David.

When I was done, she continued to eat while she watched a hummingbird flit around a bright red feeder. I picked a piece of apple out of the chicken salad and popped in in my mouth, waiting. Aunt Jewel liked to take her time mulling things over.

"Is there a chance?" Aunt Jewel asked at last, turning to look at me. The little rhinestones sewn on her shirt winked in the sunlight, and her eyes were sharp behind her glasses. "Any chance at all that with this girl's help, you could find David and stop him from sending people after you? Or whatever awful thing it is that's supposed to happen?"

Taking a deep breath, I fiddled with the wax paper around my sandwich. I wasn't hungry anymore, not even for Aunt Martha's chicken salad. "I think there might be, yeah," I said at last, and Aunt Jewel gave a little nod before biting into her sandwich.

"Well," she said after a moment, "then that's it, isn't it? Nothing else to be done about it."

I squinted at her, and not just because of the sun in my eyes. "Aunt Jewel," I said, setting my sandwich down on the bench beside me. "You know I can't just . . . frolic off around the country with Blythe and Bee. I'm not old enough to rent motel rooms, not to mention the fact that my parents would never sign off on some kind of epic road trip."

"Don't you have some kind of magic for that?" she asked, waving one hand, her rings nearly blinding me. All of my aunts loved their sparkles, but Aunt Jewel had especially glittery taste. I guess that's what happens when your parents name you Jewel.

Sitting back, I braced my hands on the warm stone beneath me. "Are you seriously suggesting I use magic to brainwash my parents?"

Aunt Jewel made a harrumphing sound. "I'm saying you be the girl you're meant to be," she said. "I'm saying you have a duty and a destiny and a responsibility, and you are not a girl to shirk those things."

"I'm not," I said, and to my surprise, I felt tears sting my eyes. "But . . . this could be bad. Scary. If something happened to me, after everything with Leigh-Anne . . ."

We were both quiet for a minute. I felt like we had all started to come to terms with her death, but she was always in the back of my mind when I was weighing things like this. Yes, I had a duty to David to keep him safe. But I also had a duty to my parents not to do something stupid or reckless that could get me killed.

Aunt Jewel understood that, I knew, and when she looked at me again, her green eyes were bright. "Honey, you know you are just about my favorite thing in this whole world. If anything ever happened to you, I don't know what I'd do." Her hands, when they reached out to cover mine, were papery and cool despite the heat. "But loving people means encouraging them to be their best selves. Fixing this, sorting it out, making it right . . . that's *your* best self, Harper Jane."

It was a good thing to hear. Maybe a *great* thing. My heart seemed to swell up in my chest, and I was suddenly afraid I might burst into tears right there in the Hensley Manor courtyard.

But, I reminded myself, Aunt Jewel didn't know how out of whack my powers had been lately. If she did, would she be encouraging me to go this strongly? I was pretty sure she wouldn't be.

For a second, I thought about telling her. She'd shared a lot of my secrets, after all. It would be nice to have her know this one, too. But this one felt too big, too . . . fraught, and besides, maybe, if I got closer to David, this whole thing with my powers would sort itself out. After all, wasn't it being away from him that was making me weaker? If you thought about it *that* way, wouldn't I actually be helping myself stay safe if I went after him?

Leaning forward, I threw my arms around Aunt Jewel in a hug that could've knocked her off the bench. "You're the best, you know that?" I said, breathing in her familiar perfume of baby powder and vanilla.

She hugged me back with surprising strength for a septuagenarian. "I take it that means you're gonna try?"

Pulling back, I looked at her face and smiled. "Not just try," I told her. "I'm going to do it."

Taking a deep breath, I pulled my phone out of my pocket and dialed Blythe's number.

Chapter 12

"WELL?" I SAID, turning away from the whiteboard, a purple marker in my hand. The whiteboard had been a present from my parents last Christmas, and so far, it had definitely come in handy. Granted, they'd thought I was going to use it for studying or making college decisions, but it had its Paladin uses, too. Like this handy list of pros and cons I'd whipped up for Ryan and Bee.

Unfortunately, they did not look as impressed as I'd hoped. Bee frowned, a hand coming to her mouth. "Um. Harper. Under cons do you have, 'Might get killed'?"

I looked back at the board, tapping that particular con with the end of my marker. "Well . . . yeah. I mean, it's a *possibility,* so it wouldn't be right to leave it off. Best we go into this thing with eyes wide-open, don't you think?"

Both Bee and Ryan nodded in unison, but slowly, and I got the sense that they weren't really listening to me. They'd both gone a little glassy around the eyes, and Bee was still staring at that one con, a deep V between her brows.

Turning back to the board, I put an asterisk next to "Might get killed," and added at the bottom, "Extremely low possibility as we possess both magic and superstrength."

When I looked back at her, eyebrows lifted, she just frowned more. "Your powers—" she started, but I waved a hand.

"For now, I'm fine," I said. "Which of course means the sooner we find David, the better."

I turned back to the board before she could say more about that. "Blythe said she can find David. That she has a plan," I went on, "and while she's not exactly forthcoming about what that is, it's better than the plan we have."

"Which is?" Ryan asked, eyebrows raised.

"Nothing," I reminded him. "Our plan was basically nothing."

Ryan took a deep breath, his chest expanding. "You've got me there."

Uncapping the marker again, I drew a line between the list of pros and cons and the blank part of the board. "I talked to Blythe on the phone this afternoon and told her that our main challenge is time. We don't have an indefinite amount of it to spend chasing David all over the country. School starts in four weeks, which means this road trip can take two, tops."

"Why not the full month?" Bee asked, but before I could answer, she lifted one hand. "Right, because you need two weeks to get ready for school to start."

As SGA president, I had certain school responsibilities that had to be dealt with before the year started. Helping with assigning textbooks, situating lockers, that kind of thing. Not even tracking down David could derail me from doing my duty to Grove Academy. A girl has to have balance, after all.

"So two weeks," Ryan said, his eyes moving over the whiteboard. "That seems . . . doable."

And then he took a deep breath and rose to his feet. "I can keep an eye on things here for two weeks, I think."

Bee looked up, blinking. "What?"

Ryan huffed out a breath and rubbed a hand over the back of his neck. "I'm not coming with you."

"What do you mean?" Bee asked, standing up. "Ry, we need you."

I used to call Ryan "Ry," too, and it sounded strange hearing it from Bee's mouth. Once again, I was reminded that this was from kind of a weird situation we'd all found ourselves in, even if you took the magic stuff out of it. And right now, I almost felt like I was intruding on something I wasn't supposed to be part of, which was stupid, of course. This was totally something that involved me. And yet, I found myself stepping closer to my desk, fiddling with the big calendar.

I was staring hard at July 31 as Ryan said, "You need a Mage, and you'll have one with you."

"A crazy one," Bee countered, and I had to admit she had a point there.

"Someone has to stay here," Ryan said, and when I looked up, he had his arms folded over his chest, palms cupped around his elbows. He'd lifted his chin just enough to let me know that this was one of those hills he was going to die on. He and David could go toe-to-toe in the Most Stubborn Guy I Know competition. "David made one Paladin, but he could make more. That one is gone, but who's to say another one won't come after Harper? And if she's not here? What happens then?"

I had to admit it wasn't something I'd thought about, and I was suddenly grateful for Ryan and really liked having him on my team. It was a nice thing to know, actually, that you could break up with someone and maybe like them more.

"Bee," I said, hoping I came across as gentle and not condescending, "that makes a lot of sense. I'd feel better if Ryan were with us, too, don't get me wrong, but . . . someone has to keep an eye on things here, and we need Blythe to come with us."

I was a little afraid that Bee might offer to stay with Ryan in that case, and the idea of being trapped alone in a car with Blythe for two weeks kind of made me want to die. But thank God, Bee proved, once again, that she was the best friend a girl could have.

"Ugh!" With both hands, she shoved her hair back from her face, and even though she was clearly frustrated, it was equally clear that she was coming with me. She looked at Ryan and reached out, lightly punching his arm. "Fine. Be right."

With a grin, he slung an arm around her neck and pulled her in so that he could kiss the top of her head.

"Another girl who says I'm right like it's killing her," Ryan said with a lopsided grin. "What is my problem?"

"You have excellent taste as far as I can tell," I told him briskly as I re-capped my marker. "But while you staying here is probably a good idea, I'd be lying if I said I was completely down with it."

"Because you'll miss my face?" Ryan teased, and I acted like I was going to throw my marker at him, making him laugh and jokingly duck.

"No, because we'll miss your *magic*," I replied.

"That's a good point," Bee said, chewing on her lower lip. "Blythe has some, sure, but it's not like we can trust that."

Ryan scrubbed one hand up and down the back of his neck, nodding. "Yeah, that's the only thing. I almost wish . . ." He sighed, dropping his hand. "It's stupid."

"Stupider than going off on a road trip with a girl who tried to kill me?" I asked, drumming the marker on my desk, and Ryan huffed out a laugh.

"Fair point. Okay, what I was going to say is that I wish there were some way to put a ward on the two of you. A . . . a protection mark or something."

Bee had sat back down on my bed, one leg folded beneath her. "Can you do that?" she asked. "Ward a person?"

"A magical tattoo," I mused, and Bee's head whipped toward me, eyes wide.

"Whoa, you mean like a permanent ward?"

Ryan shrugged. "Don't see why not. At least there's nothing I've ever seen saying you can't."

I didn't exactly relish the idea of getting a tattoo, trust me. It was right up there with blue hair.

"Do it," I said, holding my arm out to Ryan, whose auburn eyebrows had disappeared under his shaggy hair.

"For serious?"

Taking a deep breath, I looked at the unmarked, pale skin of my inner wrist. My parents were going to lose their minds over this, but if Ryan couldn't come with us, it made sense to at least bring the best part of him, aka his magic. Okay, maybe not the *best* part of him—that wasn't exactly fair. But the most useful part for sure.

Ryan paused for a moment, then turned to get one of the Sharpies from my desk.

"You sure about the arm?" he asked. "Might make sense to get it somewhere harder to see."

I rolled my eyes. "Oh my God, I am not getting a tramp stamp. I would literally rather die."

Ryan snorted softly at that and then tapped the end of the Sharpie against the back of my hip. "Here, then. Not right in the middle, still easy to hide with clothes."

Downstairs, I could hear my parents watching TV, the distant sound of a tennis match drifting up to my room. Next to me, sitting on the edge of the bed, Bee was fiddling with the hem of her shirt, worrying her lower lip between her teeth.

"All for one, one for all?" I suggested, and after a moment, she nodded.

"Might as well."

Ryan drew the looping mark on my back, a series of whorls and twists that didn't mean anything to me. But while I might not have been able to recognize what he was drawing, I could feel the power coming off the mark. If it felt like this when it was drawn in bright pink marker, how would I feel when it was permanently tattooed on my skin?

"This is for protection against Blythe," he said as he drew and I tried not to feel embarrassed, "and I'll give you my rose balm. For when you need to be . . . persuasive."

"We'll get these in white ink," Bee suggested as Ryan moved on to draw the mark on her hip. "The power would still be the same even if it doesn't show too much, right?"

Ryan nodded, his wavy hair falling in his eyes a bit. It was cute, and I could tell Bee thought so, too. It was there in the little smile that spread across her face, the way her eyes crinkled at the corners. Once Bee's mark was done, Ryan sat back, my desk chair creaking slightly under his weight, and the three of us looked at one another.

Smacking both palms flat on my thighs, I stood up with all the forced cheer I could manage. "Well, shall we hit the tattoo parlor, y'all?"

Just over an hour later, Bee and I left the Ink Pot with white bandages on our backs and little foil packets of ointment clutched in our hands. Underneath the bandage, the wards Ryan had made throbbed under my skin, both from the pain of the needle—seriously, that was going to be the last tattoo this gal *ever* got, ouch—and from the magic in the mark. If I'd had any doubts about this idea working, I was over them now. No matter what else, Bee and I were definitely warded, both from anything that might hurt us and from Blythe's magic, just to be on the safe side. Still, I couldn't escape the feeling that this was a little bit like putting a Band-Aid over a bullet hole. If more Paladins came after me, and if my powers stayed . . . blinky, I wasn't sure just how well a tattoo was going to protect me.

That errand done, I went back to my house—Ryan had driven Bee home—and changed into a sundress. No chance of my T-shirt riding up so they could see the bandage.

Mom got home around four, Dad an hour later, and we had dinner outside. It was still hot, but the deck was shaded by big trees, and besides, once May first hit, Dad was all about grilling. That night's offering was steak-and-vegetable kabobs, and I waited until we were nearly done—and until both my parents had had two glasses of wine, not that I'm proud about that—to tell them about the road trip plan. While I kept my hand from straying to the mark on my hip, I leisurely applied the rose balm to my lips, then made sure to touch Mom's hand as I said something, to let my fingers brush Dad's when I brought him a glass of iced tea. I used words like "college" and "bonding experience" and "totally supervised." I made sure to tell them how there were already three other girls on the waiting list for my job at the pool. But I didn't give any details, and as I finished up, I waited for them to say some variation of "Hell to the no."

No matter how often I'd seen magic work like this, I never fully believed it *would*. So once my little spiel was done, I was one hundred percent prepared for this to blow up spectacularly.

Instead, to my surprise, they both smiled at me in a slightly dazed way that had nothing to do with the wine and everything to do with Ryan's balm.

"That sounds nice," Mom said.

"A really good idea," Dad agreed, nodding.

It was what I'd wanted, obviously. The last barrier to finding David, gone.

So why did I feel so guilty?

But before I had time to stew in too much angst, my phone chimed in my pocket, signaling a text from Blythe. There were logistics to figure out and discussions to have.

And one truly terrifying road trip to plan.

Chapter 13

WE LEFT early in the morning, wanting to get as much time on the road as we could. The sooner this whole thing got started, the sooner it would be over.

Still, even though I wasn't looking forward to two weeks in a car with Blythe, there was a part of me that was actually . . . excited? A road trip after months of sitting at home seemed like just the thing I needed, and after so long just *waiting*, it felt really good to be *doing* something.

So, yeah, I had felt a little giddy as I'd packed last night and possibly made a few mixes for Appropriate Quest Music.

Blythe met us at my house. I had no idea where she'd come from or how she'd gotten there, but she was wearing a loose sundress, an admittedly super cute bag at her feet. Big sunglasses covered her face, and she gave me a tight smile as Bee and I made our way to her.

"You two ready?"

Bee and I had matching Vera Bradley bags—gifts from our parents for 4.0 GPAs sophomore year—we'd picked them out together. I pressed a button on my key fob, opening the trunk. "Ready as we'll ever be," I said, tossing my bag in. Bee followed suit, and after a pause, so did Blythe. To anyone passing by, we were just three girls headed off somewhere. Probably Panama City Beach, where we'd wear bright bikinis and try to con older guys into buying us drinks. Instead, we were two Paladins and a Mage, going on a quest to save an Oracle.

Despite how scary this whole thing was—and trust me, it was way scary—I mean . . . come on. It was kind of awesome, too. And really, how often do you get to actually *quest* in this day and age? And I'd have Bee with me, which meant everything. There had been a time I'd been afraid I'd never see Bee again, and yet here she was, at my side.

Of course, the reason I'd almost lost Bee forever was standing right in front of me, which made it harder to believe this was a good idea. But it was the only idea we had, and I was determined to see it through.

I'd said good-bye to Mom and Dad inside, and I was in a hurry to get going. So was Blythe, I thought, watching her drum her nails on the roof of my car.

But Bee was still standing there, stretching up on her tiptoes to look down the street. "Ryan said he was coming," she explained, "and I told him to be here early."

"Ryan's 'early' is a little different from how the rest of us would define it," I told her, trying to stamp down my impatience.

Last night, I had met Blythe back at the Waffle Hut, and we'd gone over where we were heading. She'd unfolded a map on the table, ignoring the sticky spots where syrup hadn't been totally cleaned up, and pointed to a spot in north Mississippi. "Here first," she said, tapping a place so tiny it didn't even have a name.

I had taken a sip of Coke—the regular kind this time. Planning requires both sugar *and* caffeine. "What's there?" I asked.

Blythe had wrinkled her nose at me and tapped the spot again. "Trust me, okay? We can talk about it when we get there."

"Why not now?" I'd asked. "Because you feel like being mysterious, or because you know that I won't want to go if you tell me?"

This time, I got an eye roll in addition to the nose wrinkle. "Can you just trust me?"

"No," I'd replied immediately, and to my surprise, she'd smiled.

Sitting back in the booth, Blythe had watched me for a long moment. Her dark hair had been loose for once, and it made her look younger. I had to remind myself that I hardly knew anything about her. Maybe she was *my* age. Another teenage girl caught up in something she didn't understand, but one who, I think we can all agree, had really run with it.

"Has it occurred to you," she asked, leaning forward to rest her arms on the table, "that I'm putting a lot of trust in you, too? I mean, I'm getting into a car with a *Paladin* and her best friend, both of whom have more than enough reasons to want to hurt me. So can we just make a deal to trust each other the best we can, and stop thinking the other is looking for a backstabbing opportunity?"

"Literally," I'd quipped, and while she hadn't exactly offered her hand for us to shake on it, I felt like a deal had been made.

So I hadn't pressed her any more. It was my car we were taking, after all, and while I wasn't sure I believed that Blythe wanted to help out of the goodness of her heart, I believed that she wanted to undo what she'd done the night of Cotillion.

I was distracted from that line of thinking by the sound of a car turning down our street. It wasn't Ryan's SUV, though. It was Aunt Jewel's massive Cadillac, and I grinned to see it. I'd hoped to get a chance to say good-bye to her, and when I saw that Ryan was in the passenger seat, I smiled even more. She must have gone by to pick him up on her way over.

The giant Cadillac careened to a stop at the end of the driveway, and I grimaced as Aunt Jewel's bumper took out one of our trash cans.

The car parked, she got out, wearing yet another rhinestone-studded sweater, this one in a pale pink with matching slacks. She was holding a plastic Piggly Wiggly sack, and I went around to her side of the Cadillac, giving Bee and Ryan a little bit of privacy on the other side.

"I knew that boy would be late if left to his own devices, so I decided to swing by and get him myself," Aunt Jewel said, taking my proffered hand and hefting herself out of the driver's seat. "I can still do that, right? Even though y'all aren't together anymore?"

She didn't even wait for me to answer, instead thrusting the Piggly Wiggly bag at me.

"Here, baby."

I took the shopping bag and glanced inside. A rainbow of Tupperware stared back at me, along with several plastic sandwich bags, all holding, as far as I could tell, different types of cookies.

Reaching in, I lifted one napkin-wrapped bundle and held it up to my aunt, my eyebrows raised. "Um. Cake?"

Aunt Jewel shrugged and fiddled with the appliqué hummingbird on her shirt. "You girls will get hungry, and Lord only knows what you'll find to eat out there. I figured better safe than sorry. And your aunt May went ahead and put her best cooler in the trunk, so make sure you grab that, and if you'll just stop and pick up some bags of ice—"

I threw my arms around her before she finished, squeezing tight.

"I love you, Harper Jane. And I want you to promise me you and these girls are going to be very careful. And call me every night."

"Every night," I vowed, grateful for about the hundredth time that I'd decided to tell Aunt Jewel my secret.

Ryan and Bee had apparently said their good-byes, because they crossed around to the front of the car, their arms around each other's waists. Blythe stood off alone but didn't seem all that self-conscious. That wasn't a surprise, I guess, seeing as how being self-conscious probably required an amount of self-*awareness* I doubted Blythe possessed.

"So how long will y'all be gone?" Aunt Jewel asked, and I stood up a little straighter.

"Two weeks. We'll be back by the end of the month."

Reaching down, Aunt Jewel plucked at her lace collar. "And if you don't find David?"

"We come back anyway," I said, enjoying how resolutely I said that. I just wished I felt as resolute. If all of this ended up being for nothing, if I sent myself traveling all over who knew where just to come home empty-handed . . .

No. Thinking like that had to stop. We had two weeks, and in that time, we were going to find David, find out what had happened to him, and stop it from happening anymore.

Somehow.

For now, I just gave Aunt Jewel another hug, and then, as Bee went to hug her, too, I turned to Ryan.

He stood there in another T-shirt and his basketball shorts, familiar as always, his hands held out to his sides. "Do we, uh, do we hug?"

I punched him lightly in the bicep and then wrapped my arms around his shoulders, giving him what was basically the most platonic hug known to man.

When we pulled back, he met my eyes, hands braced on both my shoulders. "You remember?" he asked in a low voice, and I glanced over at Bee, trying to keep my hand from straying to the bandage still taped over the tattoo on my back. It was just a ward, for the most part, but Ryan had added something extra to mine, something that could only be activated with a certain collection of words he'd taught me.

Something Bee didn't know about.

I turned back to Ryan and nodded. "I won't have to use it."

"Let's hope," he answered, and then moved away from me.

Our good-byes said (and Aunt May's cooler packed in the trunk), Bee, Blythe, and I got in my car. I looked at my house in the morning sunlight and told myself that I should feel excited. Anticipatory. Other words that weren't "scared out of my mind" and "freaked out."

Bee clearly felt the same because she reached over and gave my hand a quick squeeze. "We've totally got this," she told me, and I made myself smile back.

"Of course we do."

Starting the car, I glanced back at Blythe. "What about you, Blythe? You got this?"

"I *told* you," she said, tapping her chest. "I can feel the spell we're going to need. You help me find him, I'll help you fix him."

"Awesome," I muttered, plugging the address she'd given me last night into my phone's GPS. "So here we go."

And there we went.

The motel attendant looked like Harper.

But then it seemed like every girl looked like Harper lately, that he saw her heart-shaped face and green eyes on everyone who crossed his path.

As the clerk turned away, tapping something into the computer, David closed his eyes, sucking in a deep breath.

"If we go to prom, do you promise not to wear pastel?"

They're in his bedroom, Harper sitting primly at his desk chair while he slouches against the bed, a book on his upraised knees. He looks at her and feels that giddy drop in his stomach he gets every time he remembers she's his girlfriend. That if he wants to, he can get up and walk over to her, drop a kiss on her lips, slide his fingers under the heavy, silky hair that falls against her neck.

Harper Price. Pres.

His girlfriend.

It's still such a weird thing to think that he almost misses her question, and when she just looks at him, eyebrows raised, he mimics her expression. "Pastel is off the menu, too?" he finally asks, then gives her the most serious frown he can muster. "First plaid, then stripes, now pastel?" Shaking his head, David closes the book with a thump. "You're a fashion tyrant, you know that, Pres?"

Harper smiles, making a dimple dent one cheek, and there's that stomach swoop again. Reaching over to his desk, she picks up a pen, tossing it at him. "You love it," she counters.

I love you, *he thinks, but doesn't say it.*

"Are you okay?"

Startled, David raised his eyes back to the motel clerk. His head still felt full of Harper, but looking at the girl in front of him now, the resemblance wasn't as strong. Still, his pulse seemed to speed up, and there was that feeling in his chest, a tightness like someone was reeling in a line looped around his heart.

She was coming for him.

Hands shaking, David fumbled with his wallet. He wouldn't run from her. He would wait here, let her find him, let them end this, whatever it was. Maybe he could just go back. Harper wanted to keep him safe. Some part of his mind balked at that idea, but that wasn't *him*. Not the real him, at least. That was the

Oracle part, and it was the Oracle part that he had to fight. Sure, there had been the girl at the fast-food place, then before her, those girls in Alabama, but those had been accidents. Besides, once he'd come back to himself, he'd been able to pull the power from them, change them back into what they were.

Or at least he thought he had. He'd *tried*.

But when he closed his eyes—just for a second, trying to get his thoughts to settle—there were other voices in his head again. Other images.

Stand and fight, they whispered, the voices bleeding together. He'd heard these voices before, but it seemed like they were louder now, stronger.

He opened his eyes.

The girl in front of him was looking at him funny, and David knew he must be mumbling to himself again. He'd been concentrating so hard on keeping his eyes downcast—so she couldn't see the glow through his glasses—that he forgot about what his mouth was doing. That was another thing, the way he couldn't seem to control everything at once. He could talk but not look, look but not talk. And when he looked, half the time, he wasn't seeing the person in front of him but . . .

Her name.

She had a name, the girl he was seeing. He had just thought it, had just held the name inside his mind, he was sure of it, but it was slipping away now, almost like it had never been there at all.

Paladin.

No, that wasn't her name; it's what she was.

The money tumbled from his hands, bills falling to the

grubby carpet, change clattering against the desk. He was on his knees, and the pain in his head was a hurricane.

Yellow dress. Blood. Green eyes. Green eyes filled with tears, and a word booming around loud as thunder.

Choose.

The girl behind the desk was next to him now, crouching down. She smelled like strawberries, and her hair brushed his shoulder. It was brown hair, not black, but he could still swear it was that other girl next to him. The one whose name had slipped through his fingers like sand.

The last time the light poured out of him, he'd said he was sorry. He'd felt sorry.

He didn't feel sorry now.

Chapter 14

I WONDERED HOW long it would take Blythe to notice that I wasn't driving toward the address she'd given me. I had banked on her not being all that familiar with this area—we had no idea where she was from, but Blythe was a Yankee name if I'd ever heard one—so I figured it would take a while.

As it turned out, we were nearly to my destination before Blythe suddenly twisted in her seat and said, "Wait, why aren't we on the interstate yet?"

"Because we're not getting on the interstate," I answered calmly, signaling to turn right onto a long four-lane highway bracketed with palm trees. We were farther south now, which meant the landscape was slowly sliding into beachy territory, white sand appearing between clumps of dark green grass.

Blythe turned to face me, frowning. "What's going on?"

"A mutiny," Bee said cheerfully from the backseat, and I gave an unapologetic shrug. "What she said."

I was willing to concede that Blythe had something we needed, namely a bunch of magic Ryan didn't know, plus what appeared to be a genuine desire to fix this mess with a specific spell. But that didn't mean that I was giving her total control of this mission, no matter what she might think. We could follow her plan when the time came, but for now, there was a stop *I* wanted to make.

We passed a big wooden "Welcome to Piedmont" sign, and Blythe settled back in her seat with a huff, crossing her arms over her chest. "We're going to see the girl who attacked you," she said, and I nodded.

"The night she went after me, she was totally set to kill me until she *wasn't*. I know from experience that Paladin fights don't work like that. You fight—"

"Until you're dead," Blythe finished. "Yeah, I'm familiar with all that."

Ignoring her snotty tone, I turned into the wide parking lot of a strip mall. There was one just like it in every town in Alabama, seemed like, and I could see that was true of Mississippi, too. A nail salon, a Chinese buffet, one of those places where you trade your car title for cash . . .

The store I was looking for was on the very end of the row, a knockoff card and gift boutique with lots of brightly colored quilted bags prominently displayed in the window.

According to the research I'd done (by which I mean I used Google for about twenty minutes), this was where Annie Jameson worked. It had been a real find, discovering her job, tucked into a little article about her when she'd been the Piedmont High Star Student Athlete. Rocking a 4.0 GPA and captaining her volleyball team, Annie also worked afternoons at her family's boutique, according to the paper. I had no idea if she'd be there today, of course, but I figured it was easier to try to talk to her at her work than going to her house.

You should always plan the approach that will bring you the most success. I read that in an ACT prep book, but it seemed applicable here, too.

"So what are we going to do?" Blythe asked as we got out of the car. "Just walk up there, be like, 'Hi, my crazy ex-boyfriend gave you superpowers, and I'd like to ask you some questions about that'?"

The sun was beating down, and I could feel sweat popping out on my forehead, but I shrugged. "More or less, yeah."

Shaking her head, Blythe slammed the car door way harder than was necessary. "And you didn't tell me about this why?"

"Oh, I don't know," I said, adjusting my purse on my shoulder. "Maybe because you haven't exactly been forthcoming, yourself?"

Blythe started to say something to that, but I cut her off with a raised hand. "No. I need you, but you need me, too, or you wouldn't have come to me in the first place. So we'll work together, but if you're going to work your agenda, I'm going to work mine, too."

A muscle in Blythe's jaw twitched, and her lips clamped tight together, but after a moment, she shrugged, sliding her sunglasses down her nose. "Fair enough."

That settled, I turned to start walking to the store, Bee right beside me. "What *are* you going to say to her?" she asked, her voice pitched low. "Is she even going to know who you are?"

"I don't know," I replied, answering both questions.

The paper had mentioned her being confused, having only

vague memories of what had happened, so for all I knew, she was going to stare at us blankly and this entire detour would be pointless.

I wasn't sure what bugged me more, the idea of not getting answers from her or the thought of how smug Blythe would be if it didn't work out.

And sure enough, from behind me, Blythe piped up, "She's probably not even here. She was just in the *hospital*."

That was true and a good point. I had no reason to assume that Annie would be at the store today, but that Star Student Athlete piece made me think that Annie might be a kindred spirit in overachieving . . . and if it were *me* . . . Yeah, I'd be back at my parents' boutique, trying to get back to normal as quickly as possible.

Pushing open the door to the boutique, I put on my brightest smile and prepared to do my best Polite Southern Girl to whoever might be behind the counter, whether it was Annie Jameson or not.

But it turned out my gamble was right on because, sure enough, Annie stood right inside the door. She wasn't behind the counter, but was instead next to a display of pretty, brightly colored glass bottles.

She turned to us, a smile already in place, and then I got a definitive answer as to whether or not she remembered me.

Barely missing a beat, Annie grabbed the nearest glass bottle and chucked it at my head.

I ducked fast and dimly heard the glass explode somewhere behind me, but Annie was already running, and so was I. She headed around the counter, and without thinking, I placed one hand on it, vaulting over easily and catching her arm just as she tried to slam the door to the stockroom.

We fell to the floor hard, and I tried my best to keep a firm grip without hurting her. Whatever Paladin powers she'd had that night at the pool, I could sense that they were gone now. Even though I wanted answers, I wasn't about to go all Paladin on someone who couldn't fight back.

"I'm sorry!" she was saying—nearly sobbing it, actually. "It wasn't my fault, I didn't mean to—"

I'd managed to get her pinned underneath me, being careful not to sit on her or hold her arms too hard. "Annie," I said, trying to make her listen, but her big blue eyes were wild, rolling from side to side, clearly looking for someone to help her.

"I'm not here to hurt you," I said, and she looked up at me, brow wrinkled.

"I . . . I tried to kill you," she said, and I eased my grip on her arms just the littlest bit.

"I know this is hard to believe, but I'm not here for revenge or anything," I answered, trying to keep my voice calm. But it was all too easy to remember that this girl had come really close to killing me. To hurting Bee.

I could swear my scalp still stung from where she'd grabbed my hair, and I gritted my teeth, reminding myself yet again not to hold her too hard.

"I just have a few questions, and I'd really like them answered," I said, and from behind me, Blythe suggested, "We could tie her up?"

Annie started to struggle again at that, and I shot Blythe a glare. "Not. Helpful."

Turning back to Annie, I lifted one hand from her arm, holding my palm out flat. "If I let you up, do you promise not to freak out?"

Annie's blue eyes shot to Blythe again, but after a second, she nodded, and I slowly eased back.

"My mom went to get lunch," Annie said, wiping her nose with the back of her hand as she sat up. "She'll be back really soon."

"And we'll be gone before that," I promised her. "I just need to know about what happened the other night."

What had happened, turned out, was something like I'd thought. David had come in the shop, seeming confused and lost. He'd been wearing sunglasses, Annie told us, but he took those off, and then . . .

"Light," she said now, leaning against the wall of the storage room. "Like, this golden, overwhelming light, and after that . . ." Trailing off, she shook her head. "It's all kind of fuzzy. I remember seeing your face in my mind." She nodded at me. "And suddenly, I knew all these words. Paladin, Oracle . . . I knew all these *things* . . ." Her gaze got a little hazy, and she lifted one hand to her mouth, chewing at her fingernails. "It was the weirdest thing. One minute, I was here, everything the same as it's always been. The next, it's like I was on this quest, and nothing made sense but everything made sense?"

I thought of how I'd felt that first night, fighting Dr. DuPont in the bathroom. It had been like that. Like I'd just been plucked out of one life, and dropped into another, but somehow knew exactly what to do.

So I nodded and Annie continued. "I remember getting in my car. I have these flashes of fighting with you, of feeling like I *had* to fight you."

None of that was surprising, so I just filed it all away to process later. David had made her and he'd sent her after me on purpose. It's not like I hadn't thought that was probably the case, but there was a huge difference between suspecting something and knowing it flat out.

"But you stopped," I said to her, crossing my arms over my chest. "That's not usually the deal."

"He made me stop," she said simply, and my heart thudded hard in my chest.

"What?"

Sighing, Annie straightened up from the wall. "It was like I heard his voice in my head, and he was screaming at me to stop."

Her eyes met mine. "The Oracle," she clarified. "Or . . . I don't know, it sounds weird—"

"Everything sounds weird with this," Bee reminded her. She was standing near the door, occasionally casting one eye back toward the shop, but no one had come in yet. Of course, when I glanced at the clock, I realized we'd been here less than fifteen minutes.

Annie gave a little laugh and took a deep breath. "True," she acknowledged with a nod. "Okay, in that case . . . the Oracle sent me after you." She looked at me again, her eyes meeting mine. "The Oracle wanted me to kill you."

I swallowed hard. "Right."

"But the person he is—whoever he is *besides* that whole Oracle part? That's the voice I heard in my head, I think. It's like . . . it's like he's two people, I think. The Oracle who wants to kill you, and the regular guy who wants you to be okay."

It was small comfort, really, but it was *something*. It meant that David was still in there, was still fighting the Oracle half of himself.

Blowing out a long breath, I nodded. "Thank you, Annie," I said, "Really. Only a few hard feelings about you trying to scalp me."

We'd gotten the answers we came for, and I could hear the beep of the alarm system as someone—Annie's mom, no doubt—opened the back door, calling out, "Annie?"

Blythe and Bee were already heading out into the main part of the boutique, and I turned to follow them, but before I could, Annie caught my arm.

Turning back, I raised my eyebrows and she added, "Part of him loves you." She tightened her grip. "But trust me—the part that wants you dead is stronger."

Chapter 15

Once upon a time, I had been SGA president and head cheer-leader. I'd been a Homecoming Queen and a beauty contestant.

Safe to say, I hadn't expected to spend *any* night in a no-tell motel in Mississippi, yet that was exactly where I found myself.

"Oh God, Harper, no," Bee said from the passenger seat, but Blythe leaned forward, squinting at the neon sign. "This'll do," she said, and I looked at Bee with an apologetic shrug.

"It's cheap," I reminded her as I applied a fresh layer of rose balm to my lips. "And just for one night. Plus if anyone is look-ing for us, who would look here?"

Bee grimaced, ducking her head to look through the wind-shield at the long rectangle of aqua-and-cream brick stretching out in front of us. "It's actually a relief to think that no one would ever look for us here," she admitted, and I cracked a smile.

"Our reputations are safe," I said, and Bee rolled her eyes, but opened her door.

We'd headed north after our stop in Piedmont, and all of us were tired and lost in our own thoughts. I think Blythe was still put out that I hadn't told her about going to Piedmont in the first place, and I kept mulling over what Annie had told me. It may be good to know part of David was still there, but I believed her about the Oracle part being stronger.

Believed her, and had no idea what to do about it.

The sun was already beginning to set as we opened the door labeled "of ice." The girl behind the desk was about our age, with mousy brown hair that hung just past her collarbone. She was reading a romance novel with "Billionaire" in the title, one that Mrs. Morrison back at Hensley Manor would no doubt approve of.

Ryan's magical balm had worked with my parents, but then we'd used magic on them before.

Affecting the most mature expression I could manage, I leaned nonchalantly on the counter. "We need a room?"

The girl—her name tag read "Shelley" in white letters—didn't even look up from her book. "Fifty dollars for a double," she said in a bored voice, and when I pulled my wallet out of my bag, she fished out a form, sliding it over to me.

I signed the piece of paper that promised I wasn't going to trash the place, and as I did, I could feel the weight of Shelley's gaze on me. I lifted my head, meeting her eyes, but as soon as I did, she ducked her gaze back down to her book, one finger twirling her hair.

It couldn't have been clearer that Shelley was totally bored, and I told myself I was just being paranoid. If another Paladin chick was going to come after me, she wouldn't be here waiting. We'd picked this place on impulse, so how could anyone know where we'd be?

They could if they could see the future, moron, a not-very-nice part of my brain whispered.

I swallowed hard before reminding myself about positive thinking again. Even if David was conjuring up Paladins, he had called Annie off, right? Shelley handed me a key card—I was honestly surprised a place this trapped in 1993 had key cards—and pointed to her right. "One thirty-two is on the end," she said, "but not, like, the *end*."

"Awesome, thanks!" I said, probably way too brightly.

Blythe and Bee had hung back during this little exchange, and while Bee was texting, Blythe was watching Shelley with the same suspicion I'd felt.

I didn't like it.

Not that Blythe was suspicious, but that we might have something in common.

"We're on the end," I told them. "'But not, like, the end.'"

"The hell does that mean?" Blythe asked, shifting her bag to her other arm.

"Guess we'll find out."

The three of us made our way down the cracked sidewalk outside the building. Off to my left, the sun was a blazing orange ball, just about to set. We'd been driving for what felt like forever, and I was very, very glad that this day was ending.

I was also very glad a shower was in my future.

Room 132 was indeed at the end but not, like, the end, and I saw exactly what Shelley had meant. The rooms at the *end* end were blocked off with yellow tape.

Fabulous.

I slid the key into the door, and swung it open.

"Oh, good," I said as we stood in the doorway. "I'd been afraid the room would be really depressing."

At my side, Bee gave a little snort of laughter. Or maybe that was her trying to cover a sob. I felt a little sobby myself looking at that room.

Two double beds took up most of the room; both were covered in bedspreads the same bright aqua as the bricks outside. I'd never thought of aqua as being a particularly offensive color before, but looking at those bedspreads, I knew that next school year I was totally banning anything even approaching that shade from any school dance decorations. I'd never be able to look at it again without wanting to slit my own throat.

Moving into the room, I looked for a place to set my bag where it wouldn't possibly pick up some kind of insect. I settled for the battered desk, and Bee did the same.

Blythe apparently had no such issues with the room, though, because she cheerfully tossed her bag on one of the beds and flopped into a seated position, pulling her legs up under her.

I wasn't sure if she was doing yoga or just recharging her evil.

Bee blinked twice and then said, "I'm . . . gonna go call Ryan."

Retrieving her cell phone from her pocket, she stepped outside, leaving me with Blythe. I waited until I heard Bee's footsteps recede, then gingerly made my way over to the other bed. I needed to call my parents and Aunt Jewel, but I didn't want to do that with Blythe in the room, and for some reason, I didn't want to leave her by herself.

I know that sounds stupid, but there was no telling what

Blythe might get up to her on her own. So for now, I would just stay here and . . . watch her.

You know, in a non-creepy way.

She sat still on the middle of the bed, her legs folded, hands resting on her knees. She was taking deep breaths through her nose, and I didn't want to disturb her but I also wanted to know what the heck she was doing.

"So are you resting, or . . ."

"Why don't you go grab a shower?" Blythe suggested, not answering my question.

"Omigod, I don't smell, do I?" I picked at the collar of my T-shirt, giving a discreet sniff inside. I'd been using all the deodorant, so I was pretty sure I was Powder Fresh, but a day in a car during a southern summer can defeat the best of us.

From her spot on the bed, Blythe smiled. "No, I just want you to leave me alone so I can try to sense the Oracle."

I felt a glimmer of relief. "Can you feel him now?"

There was a little wrinkle between her brows, but Blythe still didn't open her eyes. "No. Or I can, but it's . . . faint." I watched her take another deep breath, then another, and the frown deepened. "It's like another heartbeat inside my chest," she said, "but a really soft, fluttery one. I can only feel it when I sit still."

"I feel that, too," I said, picking at the strap of my sandal. "Not all the time, but sometimes. Like, I get this feeling that he's almost in the next room or something, but . . ." Trailing off, I rolled my eyes at myself. This was not the time to have some kind of slumber party moment with Crazy Blythe.

But then she opened her eyes. They were brown like Bee's, but a shade darker, so dark that I could hardly separate the pupil from the iris. Weird as it sounds, I'd almost expected her eyes to glow when she looked at me. Maybe that's because sitting so still and kind of pained, she'd reminded me of how David looked when he had visions.

"And the dreams?" she asked.

Startled, I raised my eyebrows. "Dreams?"

Nodding, Blythe shook out her hair. "You and Bee are having them, right? Vague things, but definitely his?"

Just last night, I'd had another one, that same weird mix of blood on a yellow dress, my voice echoing around me.

I didn't give Blythe an answer, but she went on like I had. "The closer we get, the stronger they'll become, so be sure you tell me whenever you have one."

"So we could've tracked him without you?" I said, crossing my arms. "By following our dreams?"

Blythe shrugged. "It's not exactly as precise as the magic I can do tracking him, but I guess so."

Rolling my eyes, I looked up at the ceiling. "Things that might have been helpful to know before now," I muttered, and Blythe sighed.

"Tell me about him," she said, surprising me, and I sat up a little straighter.

"About David?" I blinked, trying to think of what I could say to her. How did I even describe David? For a second, I thought about telling her the Oracle stuff. You know, unclear visions, glowing eyes, the headaches that would make him wince in pain. But I knew that's not what she wanted. Blythe wanted to talk about David the person.

That felt easier and harder all at once.

"He's . . . smart," I said at last. "And funny, but in a vaguely obnoxious way. He has the worst taste in clothes known to man—he's never met a plaid he didn't like and subsequently abuse."

That made Blythe smile a little bit. "I seem to remember that from when the two of you came to the college."

"Oh, you mean the day you tried to kill us?" I said, scooping up a bag of chips from the little pile of gas station food we'd picked up earlier.

Blythe's smile faded immediately, replaced with a scowl. "Always bringing that up."

"It's a weird thing of mine, remembering times people tried to stab me," I admitted, leaning back against the dresser. It seemed a safer bet than sitting on the other bed or the couch. I was really regretting not bringing along some Febreze, let me tell you what.

"So what's in North Mississippi?" I asked, changing the subject as I opened the chips. They were slightly stale, and I felt like they might have been in that Chevron since the Reagan administration, but I was hungry, and salt and vinegar can cover a lot of flaws.

"It's where Saylor was from," Blythe said, still sitting on the bed in that weird yoga position, her legs folded, eyes closed.

Startled, I nearly dropped the bag of chips. "What?"

Blythe opened one eye, squinting at me. "She had to come from somewhere, you know. It's not like she just appeared, being David's Mage and stuff."

"I know that," I snapped in reply, but the truth was, I hadn't thought much about where Saylor had come from. I knew she'd kidnapped David when he was a baby, saving him from the Ephors who wanted to kill him, but I'd never wondered about who had made Saylor a Mage in the first place. Like Paladins, Mages passed down their powers, which meant there had been someone who had passed his or her powers to Saylor. Blythe had willingly taken those powers on, but had Saylor been like me? Wrong place, wrong time, suddenly all magicked up?

And why had I never asked her?

"Don't look like that," Blythe said on a big sigh, stretching out her legs. "It's not like you and Saylor had a lot of bonding time before she was killed."

"Thanks to you," I couldn't help but point out. Blythe's mind control potion was responsible for turning Bee's dim bulb of a boyfriend, Brandon, into a killer. I hadn't forgotten that, either, and from the way the corners of her mouth turned down a little bit, I'm guessing Blythe hadn't.

"Collateral damage," she said, and I crumpled the bag of chips in my hand.

"Really?" I said, my voice nearly cracking with anger. "That's all you have to say about that?"

Now Blythe opened both eyes, staring at me. Her face was so innocent and sweet, but those eyes were old. They always had been.

"Would it do any good for me to say that I was sorry? That I was caught up in doing what I thought was the right thing, and that I couldn't let myself think about the people who got hurt? Would that make you suddenly trust me?"

I didn't have an answer for that. Or at least not one I wanted to say out loud. The truth was, this whole thing was so confusing that it would've been *nice* to trust Blythe. To put the past behind us and try to understand why she'd done what she had.

Instead, I threw the now-crushed chips into the trash can and picked up the ice bucket, needing to be anywhere that wasn't this room with this girl right now.

"If Bee gets back, tell her I went to get ice," I said, without looking at Blythe, but before I got to the door, she slid off the bed, coming to stand between me and escape.

"We're more alike than you want to admit, Harper," she said, reaching out to poke me in the sternum. I swatted her hand away but didn't try to push past her.

"I am sorry, for whatever it's worth," she said, and I felt my heart pounding in my ears, remembering Saylor lying on the floor of Magnolia House, her blood slick on the tile of the kitchen. Blythe might not have wielded the knife, but Saylor's death was still on her hands.

"I was trying to do the right thing," Blythe said again, and there was something in her voice that made me pause. God knew I'd screwed up enough trying to do what I thought was the right thing. No one had gotten killed, but that might have just been a matter of luck at this point.

"And yeah," she continued, "maybe I was trying to help myself, too, but aren't we the same there?"

When I just looked at her, Blythe lifted her eyebrows and said, "Think about it, Harper. Is it David you're trying to save with all of this or yourself?"

The words made my mouth go dry, and I just shook my head at her, muttering, "Whatever."

There was another pause, but after a second, she moved out of the way, and I opened the door, stepping out into the night.

Chapter 16

THE MOTEL BREEZEWAY was dim, fluorescent lights overhead buzzing as I made my way toward the vending machines, ice bucket in hand. I tried not to think too much about the stains on the concrete or where they might have come from. We had enough money—and enough magic—to stay somewhere nicer, but when you're in the middle of nowhere Mississippi, you take what you can get, and this was the only motel for miles. Still, between the patches of darkness from blown bulbs, the persistent hum of traffic from the interstate, and the stifling heat of the night, it felt like I'd stumbled into a bad horror movie. If my mom or, God forbid, The Aunts, could see me now, I'd be on the way back to Pine Grove before I could so much as spit.

David, I reminded myself. *You're doing this for David.*

But was I really? Blythe asked if this was about saving David or saving *me.* But weren't they one and the same?

The fact that I was having trouble answering that question bugged me more than it should have, and even though the night was sticky hot, I wrapped my free arm around myself like I was cold.

It was just the first day, though, and I'd been driving for hours. Of course I was tired and out of sorts. Anyone would be, and I'd never been the type to do well without sleep. The sooner I got some ice and got back to the room, the sooner I could sleep and reorientate myself.

I moved faster, passing my car. Bee was in there, sitting in the passenger seat, her feet braced on the dashboard, a big smile on her face.

So Ryan was okay, then. I waggled my fingers at her as I passed, but she didn't see me.

The vending machines were in a dim alcove past the creepy police-tape rooms, and I made my way there as quickly as possible, wishing I hadn't stormed out so quickly. Blythe was irritating and all, but surely no more irritating than getting horribly murdered would be.

"Stupid," I muttered to myself. "You are not going to be murdered unless it's death by giant mosquito."

Placing the bucket under the little plastic funnel, I pressed the button for ice. It rattled down and all that noise had to be why I didn't hear her coming. All I had was the sudden sense of someone to my right and then a blur of motion.

But this time, unlike the night at the pool, my powers were strong as ever. Grabbing the edges of the bucket, I flung the contents at Shelley—of course it was freaking Shelley, Shelley with her billionaire romance novels and that look I knew I'd felt.

The ice hit her directly in the face, slowing her down just enough for me to drop and sweep out a leg, catching her under the ankles. It was a move I went to a lot, and one that, in my experience, almost always worked. Sure enough, she hit the pavement hard.

This is one of the most important parts of a fight, gaining the higher ground, and because I was short, I always had to get higher ground as fast as possible.

But there is one problem with gaining the higher ground, and that's that you make a fairly easy target.

Shelley had barely landed when she lashed up and out with one leg, kicking me so hard in the thigh—the same spot Annie had hit that night in the locker room—that my leg threatened to buckle under me.

I gritted my teeth, falling back on my stronger leg, and . . .

Look, I've done a lot of things in my job as Paladin. I've head-butted dudes and fought while wearing formal gowns and nearly jujitsu-ed my then-boyfriend into an early grave. But kicking someone in the ribs while she was down?

Not one of my proudest moments.

Still, I was desperate and not because I was still shaken from the fight at the pool.

My powers weren't as strong as they should have been. They weren't as weak as they were that night, don't get me wrong—I was still kicking with the best of them—but they weren't anywhere near what they *had* been, and that rattled me. Besides, the sooner I got Shelley neutralized, the sooner I could interrogate her.

So I gritted my teeth, muttered, "Sorry," and kicked.

But Shelley was a lot faster than I'd thought, and my foot

barely connected with her ribs before she was rolling away, jack-knifing her body, and leaping back to her feet.

Great.

In that case, we could fight and talk.

"Why are you doing this?" I asked, dodging a punch and throwing one of my own.

Shelley grunted as I caught her under the chin, making her teeth clack together, and I thought she wasn't going to answer. But then she shook her head, her lank hair half falling out of a ponytail. Her hair had been down earlier, so I guessed she'd put it up to fight. And when she reached out for my own hair—still loose around my shoulders—I wished I'd known I was going to get involved in a throw-down before I'd come out here.

"You have to be stopped," she said to me, and I caught her outstretched arm, pulling her close and driving an elbow hard into her hip.

The impact vibrated all the way up my arm, but Shelley's knees buckled, giving me the upper hand again. "Says who?"

Shelley shook her head, then lunged forward. I just barely kept her teeth from sinking into my forearm and I scowled, tightening my grip around her neck.

"Okay, look, I am all for doing what it takes to win a fight," I gritted out, "but biting is *gross*. Do you have any idea how filthy the human mou—ow!"

She drove her head back, her skull connecting with my sternum, and my hands dropped from around her, instinctively coming up to rub against my aching chest.

Shelley just stood there, watching me, almost bobbing on her toes. I recognized that stance—I'd used it a lot of times before. Usually just before I handed someone their backside.

"Who did this to you?" I asked. "Because you know this is something that was done *to* you, right? It's not like you just woke up like this."

Shelley smiled at me then, her teeth even and straight. "Like you don't know," she said. "You know who did this."

I did, but I needed to hear her say it.

"It was a boy, right? Blond hair, terrible fashion sense? Glowing eyes?"

"You want to hurt him," she said now, and even though that confirmed what Annie had said, my stomach still dropped.

"I don't," I told her.

Still circling, Shelley kept her eyes on me, fingers opening and closing at her sides. "I can't let you hurt him," she said, and I shook my head, holding up both my hands.

"Didn't you hear me? I don't want to hurt David—uh, the guy who did this to you—I'm trying to find him and *help* him."

But Shelley nearly snarled at that. "You want to kill him," she said, and I was shocked enough that this time, I did drop my guard, stumbling back a step.

It was apparently all the opening Shelley needed because she surged forward, and I felt my limbs go weak.

But just before she was on me, she froze. And I don't mean "went still," I mean she literally seemed to freeze in midair, one foot lifted off the ground, arms wide.

Behind her stood Blythe, her hands out, her breath coming fast.

"Are you all right?" she asked, and even though I was technically uninjured, I shook my head. I was tired and shaken, and my thoughts were in a whirl, so much so that I barely registered Blythe walking up to Shelley and putting her hands on either side of her face.

"She said he's sending Paladins after me because he thinks I want to *hurt* him. Like what Annie said."

That memory came back to me, sitting in the car after we'd first met Blythe, David telling me about his dream, the one where I was crying and killing him. I saw the vision I'd had in the fun house again, my knife at his throat, my own voice telling me I'd have to "choose."

But choose what? Hurting David could not be any further from my mind.

There was a thump, and I turned to see Shelley slumped on the pavement, Blythe's hands still pressed to her face.

"What are you doing?" I asked, and she glanced up at me.

"Undoing what your boyfriend did."

There was a slight glow around Blythe's fingers, like she was cupping her palms around a light, and Shelley made a soft noise, her eyes still closed.

"You can do that?" I asked, and Blythe snorted.

"Obvi," she replied. "It'll erase her memory, but at least—"

"No!" I cried, my hand coming down on Blythe's shoulder. "She might be connected to David. She might know where he is."

But it was too late. Shelley's eyes were already fluttering open and looking at us with total confusion. "What happened?" she muttered, her voice raspy, and then, as the pain of all my blows registered, she winced, nearly curling into a ball.

Just a regular girl again.

Blythe rose to her feet then, sighing, and I had the weirdest feeling she was relieved, and not just because Shelley was back to normal.

Chapter 17

"I'm just saying, it would have been *helpful* to talk to her before you gave her the big *Eternal Sunshine* treatment."

It was an argument Blythe and I had been having since this morning, an argument that had carried us through two highways and four counties, and I wasn't quite done having it yet.

Nor was Blythe done being irritated by it.

She was wearing sunglasses, but I could feel her rolling her eyes at me as she sat in the backseat, her arms folded over her chest like a sulky toddler.

"What would she have told you that you didn't already know?" Blythe asked, shifting in her seat. "David made her. David sent her. David wants to kill you because he's gone super mega nutbar. None of that is new information, Harper. It's exactly what we got from Annie, and this time, has to be said, it didn't look like David was in any rush to call her off."

From the passenger seat, Bee made a frustrated noise, tipping her head back. She was probably getting sick of this argument, too, I thought, but then she said, "We actually don't know any of that. We're guessing based on what Annie, and now this Shelley person, said. Why would David think Harper wants to kill him?"

Bee had missed out on everything last night, and I got the sense she felt a little guilty about it. Or maybe she was just being a good best friend, automatically taking my side.

Blythe sat up in the backseat, looking at us over the rims of her sunglasses in a move that reminded me uncomfortably of David. He'd looked at me like that more times than I could count.

"Did you miss the 'super mega nutbar' part?" she asked Bee. "He thinks she wants to kill him because of that. The nutbar—"

"Yeah, I heard," Bee said, drawing her knees up to her chest and wrapping her arms around them. "But there's no confirmation, since we didn't get to ask Shelley what she knew."

"Mmm," Blythe said, nodding. "Sure, I'll own that. But I could have done worse. I mean, what if I had helped him escape wards that were set in place to keep him safe? Now *that,* that would be something to feel bad about."

"Okay, enough," I said, feeling kind of like a kindergarten teacher. "Playing the blame game is probably not the best use of our time right now."

I could feel Bee's gaze on the side of my face but kept my eyes on the road. Look, I had forgiven her for everything that had happened with David—or at least I was really trying to—but that didn't mean it was something I wanted to talk about, especially not with Blythe in the car.

But Blythe never met an uncomfortable moment she didn't want to exploit. "Maybe if you'd been around last night, you could have gotten your own answers from Shelley," she said to

Bee. "But since you were too busy talking to your boyfriend, I guess we'll never know."

"Enough!" I snapped again, my hands tightening on the wheel of the car. At the GPS's instruction—we were finally approaching the address Blythe had given me before we'd started our road trip—we'd exited the interstate for a little town called Ideal, and I was navigating the downtown area. It reminded me of Pine Grove, and even though we'd only been gone a couple of days, I was feeling a little homesick.

Bee's voice was lower as she said, "I hate that I couldn't help last night."

"It's fine," I told her.

"And even if you could have," Blythe piped up, "your powers are just as unreliable as Harper's right now. There's no telling if you would've been any use or not."

Bee nodded, and I raised my eyes to the rearview mirror. "Shouldn't they be getting better now?" I asked, turning up the air conditioner just a smidgen. "If our powers were fading because we were far from David, the reverse should be true, right? Closer we get, stronger we feel?"

Blythe shrugged, fiddling with the hem of her skirt. "No idea. That's Paladin stuff."

I looked over at Bee, noticing that she looked a little pale, and that there were soft violet shadows under her eyes. "Dreams?" I asked in a low voice, and she startled a little.

"Yeah," she said at last, crossing her arms tight over her chest. "The same one I was having before we left yesterday. With the—"

"Yellow dress and the blood," I finished up, nodding. I'd woken up from my own nightmare this morning, my breath coming in short bursts, my heart racing. The dream wasn't exactly any clearer—I still wasn't sure what was happening in it, only that there was blood and this strange, echoing effect to the voices I'd heard, saying words I couldn't quite make out—but it had felt . . . stronger. More vivid.

From the backseat, Blythe leaned forward. "You both had the dreams? Remember the part where I said to tell me that?"

I frowned, passing a white car on my right, the needle ticking just over the speed limit. "We're telling you now," I said, and Blythe blew out a frustrated breath.

"Okay, fine. Well, the good news is, if the dreams are getting stronger, we're on the right track."

Bee twisted in her seat to look at Blythe, tucking her hair behind her ears as she did. "So you can't sense David, just the magic we need to fix him."

Adjusting her sunglasses, Blythe stared straight ahead. "I can *kind* of sense him," she clarified, "but it's not precise. Like how your dreams getting stronger is a *clue* but not an exact science. I *can* track the spell, though. It takes all three of us working together to find him, like a . . . triangulation, I guess."

Snorting, Bee turned back around. "Whatever."

I didn't want another argument, so I changed the subject.

"So we're here now because of Saylor, right?" I said to Blythe.

She made a little humming sound of agreement. "Yup. She left something here—a spell. It's sending out a signal, so it must be important."

"A signal," Bee repeated, and Blythe nodded.

"Only detectable to Mages. Well, to this Mage, at least. We're close, right?" she asked me.

I looked down. My phone rested in the center console, the map app pulled up, and according to that, we were only about a mile from a house at 562 Deer Path Lane.

Sitting up, Blythe leaned between me and Bee, peering through the windshield as we drove down a quiet residential street with big oak trees that created a median down its center. The houses looked older than the ones on my block back in Pine Grove. There were lots of low brick ranchers, the occasional two-story A-frame breaking through. It was one of these that sat at 562, a solid-looking house painted a pale yellow with olive-green shutters. A newish-looking pickup truck sat in the driveway, and a birdbath in the front yard, the stone streaked with green moss.

All in all, it was a pretty enough place, but something felt . . . off to me.

"Who lives here?" I asked, and Blythe shrugged.

"Saylor Stark."

She was out of the car then, already heading for the front door while Bee and I sat there in silence for a second. And then I was throwing open the driver's side door, catching Blythe's arm just as she started up the front walk. "Hold up," I said, keeping my voice low. "What the heck does that mean? Saylor is dead."

Blythe threw off my hand with an impatient huff. "Duh. She doesn't live here *now*. This is just where she grew up. And now it's where her brother lives."

I looked up at the house. "This is where the spell is?"

Tilting her own head back, Blythe followed my gaze, but I got the sense she was looking at something specific rather than just taking in the house as a whole. "Did you think we were going to the Great Spell Outlet Mall or something?"

Bee was behind us now and she made a disbelieving sound. "Why would Saylor have left a spell *you* could sense?"

The corners of Blythe's mouth turned down, her dimples appearing. "Okay, maybe she didn't *technically* leave it for me, but for the Mage who came after her."

"Which is Ryan," I reminded her, and now it was Blythe's turn to make a disbelieving sound.

"I told you. That boy is fine as hell, don't get me wrong." She glanced over at Bee. "Good on you for that, by the way." Her eyes slid to me. "And you, too, I guess." Shaking her head, she added, "Man, you guys really did want to make everything a thousand times more complicated than it had to be, didn't you?"

"Point, Blythe," I said through gritted teeth, and she shrugged, hair bouncing.

"Point is, when it comes to Saylor's actual heir in terms of magic, that's me. She left a spell in this house and sent out a signal for another Mage to come find it. Did Pretty Boy sense anything like this?"

It felt disloyal to shake my head, but if Ryan had ever sensed anything like this, he sure hadn't mentioned it to me. And he clearly hadn't said anything to Bee, either, because she shook her head, too.

Satisfied, Blythe gave a little nod and turned back to the door.

"If you knew there was something here," I asked, just as she raised her hand to ring the doorbell, "why not go after it before? Why wait until now?"

Blythe threw a look at me over her shoulder. "I didn't pick up on it before. Saylor must have set it up so it could only be sensed if she were dead."

That made sense. After Saylor died, Blythe had been held by the Ephors until Alexander died, too.

"And another thing," she added, pressing the doorbell harder than necessary, "I wasn't sure this was something I wanted to go after on my own. Better two half-ass Paladins than no Paladins at all."

I would've had a retort to that, but I could hear footsteps from inside and a cheerful male voice calling, "Coming!"

My mouth was dry when the door opened and a man with thick silver hair stood there in khaki shorts and a button-down shirt. Shoving his hands deep in his pockets, he looked at the three of us standing there on his doorstep with a bland smile. "Morning, ladies," he said, his voice as smooth and southern as Saylor's had been.

"Good morning," I said, feeling the need to take charge of this situation before Blythe could say anything. "We're . . . we're friends of Miss Saylor's," I started, and the man's smile became something actually genuine.

"You don't say!" And then he leaned out, looking past us to the car in the driveway. "Is she with you?"

He didn't know.

The knowledge sat so heavily in my stomach I thought I might throw up. When Saylor died, we'd done the best we could

covering it up for the rest of Pine Grove, but it had never occurred to me that there were other people waiting to hear from
her, wondering what had happened to her.

What was wrong with me that I hadn't thought of that?

"Unfortunately no," Blythe said, "but she'd asked us to stop
by and say hello."

Saylor's brother nodded, clearly disappointed, and then surprised me further by saying, "She said people might be coming
by one of these days."

He stepped back, sweeping one arm. "Why don't y'all come
on in and let's have a chat."

Chapter 18

THE INSIDE of the house was . . . interesting.

If this had been Saylor's childhood home, it was pretty clear her brother had been living here for a while, because the entire decor was straight-up Southern Male Left Alone Too Long. Lots of paintings of ducks, lots of plaid furniture, and way more taxidermied heads than I ever wanted to see.

Bob—that was Saylor's brother's name—led us into a living room that sat under the baleful gaze of a giant buck's head over the fireplace, and once we all had some tea, he sat and faced the three of us. "You girls know Saylor, huh?"

He said it casually, but I saw the look in his eyes. It was hope, and it broke my heart.

I couldn't do any kind of mind control or anything, but in that moment, I had never wished harder for a power like that because all I could think was, *Blythe, you tiny crazy person, if you tell him his sister is dead like this, I am going to kill you right in front of that painting of Baby Jesus.*

But Blythe just smiled brightly at Bob and said, "We sure do! She's a very big part of our hometown."

Bob made a sound like *humph* and then sort of sucked at his teeth. There wasn't much of Saylor in his face, although his hair was a similar shade of silver, and his eyes, like hers, were blue. Saylor's had been brighter, though, and looking at Bob's, I suddenly thought of David. His eyes were blue, too, although the last time I'd seen them, they'd been shining with the golden light of the Oracle.

Thinking of that reminded me that we weren't just here to chat with Bob in front of taxidermied animals, so I sat up a little bit, pushing my glass of iced tea away.

"Mr. Stark," I said, "you said Miss Saylor said someone might come by to pick up something she'd left here?"

He nodded. "She sure did. I think it was the whole reason she stopped by in the first place."

I'd assumed Saylor had left something before she left to go be a Mage, but Bob made it sound a lot more recent than that.

"You . . . you've talked to Saylor recently?"

Bob gave a chuckle, the ice rattling in his glass. "If you can call a year ago 'recent,' I s'pose so. She showed up last summer, first time I'd seen her in ages." Nodding toward the staircase, he added, "Spent the night in her old room, then left the next morning. Said she'd kept something here for 'safekeeping,' and that if a young lady showed up asking for it, I could give it to her." He snorted and sat his glass down on the table. "Of course, might've been helpful to tell me what the damn thing was in the first place—beg pardon—but then Saylor always was secretive."

Because she was a Mage, I thought to myself, remembering all the secrets I'd have to keep over the years.

Next to me on the sofa, Blythe was strung tighter than a wire but she managed to sound almost nonchalant as she said, "Oh, that's wonderful! Do you mind if we go fetch it?"

Bob didn't answer her but instead kept his eyes on me. I fought the urge to squirm in my seat. Was it better for him not to know the truth about Saylor? Every time I'd had to lie to anyone—from my parents to David—I'd told myself that it was because it was for the best.

But was it really? Was it my place to decide that?

Blythe cleared her throat, and Bob looked back at her. "Oh, sure," he said, gesturing with his glass up the stairs. "Go on. I take it you know what you're looking for? I figured it was jewelry or something."

Blythe just made a vague sound of agreement that had me shooting a look at her, one she pointedly ignored.

I glanced over at Bee, who gave me a little nod, and I knew she was agreeing to sit downstairs and make small talk with Bob while we did our searching. Bee was pretty good at the whole "charming adults" thing, maybe even better than me, so it seemed like a safe bet.

"Whatever it is, maybe you'll have better luck than that boy did finding it," Bob said on a sigh, and Blythe suddenly sat up a little straighter, the corner of her mouth turning down.

"Boy?" she asked, and he nodded before frowning and rubbing a hand over the back of his neck.

"Yeah, came by . . . oh Lord, I guess it was around November of last year. Said he worked for Saylor's boss, and that she'd sent him to pick up something for her. Seemed damn odd—pardon, girls, *darn* odd—but he had a business card, and . . ."

Bob's words faded away, a puzzled look on his face, and I felt something in my stomach go cold. Whoever this boy was, he'd used magic on Bob, that was for sure. I'd seen that look of confusion on people after Ryan had done his Mage thing on them. It's what Shelley at the motel had looked like when Blythe had finished with her.

And in Bob's case, who knew just how much magic had been done on him over the years? There were Saylor's spells, whoever this boy was—and what had he meant by Saylor's "boss"? Alexander? Some other Ephor before they'd all been wiped out?

I reminded myself to tell Blythe not to even attempt a mind wipe here. Lord only knew what it might do to Bob after this much magic. I wasn't even going to risk Ryan's magic rose lip balm stuff.

"What did this boy look like, if you don't mind my asking?" Blythe said, sweet as pie, and Bob's hazy eyes shot to her.

"Oh. Well. He was . . . tall? Young, not much older than you girls. Figured he was an intern or something. Asian fella, handsome as all get out."

That description wasn't familiar to me, but Blythe's lips tightened, and her hands, clasped in her lap, flexed a bit.

"Y'all need me to go up with you?" Bob asked, and we both shook our heads.

"No, we know what we're looking for," I said, even though I was pretty sure we didn't. "Won't be a tick."

The stairs creaked slightly as Blythe and I made our way up, Blythe heading unerringly for the last door on the left past the landing.

"So who was the handsome guy?" I asked, and she glanced back at me. When she didn't answer immediately, I rolled my eyes. "Oh, come on," I said. "You clearly knew who he was talking about."

Another little frown. "Dante," she answered. "Alexander's assistant . . . another Mage."

I raised my eyebrows at that. "Another one?"

"It's a long story," she replied. "And one we don't have time for now."

With that, she turned to the nearest door on her left.

"You don't know what we're looking for?" I whispered, and she tossed her hair over her shoulders, turning the doorknob.

"I'll know it when I see it."

Saylor's childhood bedroom looked a lot like . . . well, like mine. Sure, it was still solidly stuck in the 1970s, but apparently Saylor hadn't been a trend follower any more than I was. The bed was dark cherrywood, the coverlet white Battenburg lace, and other than a peeling poster of some band called Bay City Rollers—guys even more devoted to plaid than David—on the wall, there wasn't much to mark it as belonging to a teenage girl. Still, I was struck by something as I stood there, looking out the window to the empty lot across the street.

"She was normal," I heard myself say.

Blythe had already moved past me, opening drawers and rifling through them. "What?"

I glanced back out in the hall, worried that Bob would come upstairs and find us pawing through Saylor's stuff. True, we'd told him we were looking for something, but I didn't think he'd be happy with just how roughly Blythe was treating Saylor's things. I wasn't sure I was happy with it, to be honest.

"This is stupid," I whispered to Blythe even as I crossed over to a bookcase and began to looking for anything resembling a journal or a diary. "We have no idea where she could have hidden a spell. Or why she left it here, for that matter."

Snorting, Blythe moved over to the dresser. "If I had to guess, whatever it was had to do with David, and with her being worried about his powers. Think about it. She's gone for years, then suddenly turns up last summer, just when things started getting intense. Right before the Ephors found him. And besides, it's *here*. I can feel it."

"How?" I asked, picking out an old, well-thumbed copy of *Jane Eyre,* flipping through the pages. "You've said that a couple of times, but you haven't mentioned exactly what you're feeling or how you're feeling it."

Blythe paused, one hand still stuck in the dresser drawer, and I realized that she was actually attempting to formulate a serious answer rather than some mumbo jumbo or another reminder that I was totally stupid where all this stuff was involved.

"It's like . . . a homing beacon," she finally said. "Or the black boxes they put on planes. You know, like there's something . . . beeping in my head, only it's magic, not electrical." She frowned, her cherubic face wrinkling. "Does that make sense?"

I thought about the way I could still feel David, just the vaguest sense of him. Or how I'd been able to feel that he was in danger, that sensation of Pop Rocks deep in my chest.

"Yeah," I replied, sliding *Jane Eyre* back into its space. "It does, actually."

Pleased, Blythe smiled and then turned back to her rifling while I did my best to help. I definitely wasn't feeling any kind of "homing beacon," but maybe it was just a Mage thing. I'd always wished that Ryan were the Mage here with us, but, watching Blythe move around Saylor's old bedroom with the kind of efficiency usually limited to worker ants, I had to admit that she seemed pretty dedicated.

"Bob said she was just seventeen when she took off," I said as Blythe continued her search. "Same age as me."

When Blythe didn't look up, I pressed a little more. "Same age as . . . us?"

She still didn't lift her head, but her hands stilled. "Not quite. I'm nineteen."

"How long has the Mage thing been happening for you, though?" I said, leaning back against the dresser.

Blythe heaved a sigh that just ruffled her bangs, but seemed deep enough to make the curtains flutter. And then she shut the drawer, looked at me, and said, "You really want to do this now?"

I shrugged. "Why not? Seems relevant to the task at hand and all."

Blythe sighed, then shrugged herself, and said, "Fine. We can talk while we search."

Feeling more pleased with myself than I should have, I sat down on the edge of the bed. "So how long have you been a Mage?"

"I'm not one, exactly."

That startled me, although I guess it shouldn't have. The previous Mage usually has to die before another one can take over, and Blythe had powers long before Saylor had died. Ugh, this was way too much rule-breaking to take in, honestly.

"Do you have hobbies?" Blythe asked, pulling me out of my thoughts, and I shook my head, confused.

"Okay, for one, I have, like, a thousand, and two, way to change the sub—"

"Magic was my hobby," Blythe said, acting like I hadn't even spoken. "All types of magic. The traditional witches-and-broomsticks kind, the weird hippie-herbal kind . . . and then one day, I came across the Greek kind. The Mage kind. And"—she gave a little shrug, moving over to Saylor's closet—"that was clearly the most powerful kind, so that's what I wanted. Why do anything if you can't be the best at it, right?"

I really didn't like how familiar that sounded, and I fidgeted, clutching the edge of the bed. "Was that the deal with that other guy, too? This Dante kid who was here?"

Blythe nodded. "I was better, so I was the official Mage for the Ephors, but Dante wasn't . . . untalented, exactly." She flashed me a brief smile. "Just not as good as me. By that time, the Ephors needed all the help they could get, so they weren't about to let a perfectly-good-if-not-great Mage slip through their fingers."

I wanted to ask more about that, but before I could, my fingers brushed something underneath the mattress.

Dropping to my knees, I reached, my hand almost immediately touching something hard.

I tugged and was aware of Blythe coming up to stand behind me as the book slid out from between the mattress and the box springs.

Glancing up, I looked into Blythe's bright eyes and asked, "Is this what we're looking for?"

"Oh, thank God," she breathed, taking it from me.

Her fingers flew as they paged through the book, her face practically glowing.

And then, just as abruptly, her smile dropped.

There, toward the back of the book, were the jagged edges of several ripped-out pages.

Seemed Dante had found what he was looking for after all.

Chapter 19

AFTER ALL the taxidermy at Saylor's old house, I didn't think I'd ever want to eat again, but Blythe and Bee were both hungry, so we stopped in a Mexican place in the middle of what passed for "downtown."

As soon as we were situated with sweet tea and chips, Blythe pulled the journal out of her bag, and I tried not to wince as the leather hit a drop of salsa on the laminate table. "What is it?" I asked, and Bee leaned farther over the table, trying to see what Blythe was reading.

"A book," Blythe answered, and one of the chips cracked in my fingers.

"Yes, I'm aware of that," I told her. "What with it being all book-shaped and such. What I mean is what does it say, and what was it this Dante person took—"

Blythe cut me off by raising a hand and giving me a firm "Shh!"

Had someone pulled that crap on me at cheerleading practice, I'm pretty sure I would've murdered her. As it was, I was coming very close to dumping my glass of sweet tea over Blythe's head. But since a simple glance at the pages of Saylor's journal revealed the same mishmash of Greek and English we'd seen in the books at David's, I decided to let it slide so Blythe could keep reading.

I stirred a chip in the salsa while Blythe read, and at my side, Bee nudged me. "You okay?" she asked.

I wasn't sure how to answer that. On the one hand, we'd found what we were looking for. On the other, I still felt weirdly . . . disappointed.

When Blythe had said she'd had a "sense" of where we should go next, I'd hoped it would be a direct line to David. That we could find him and . . . fix him. Whatever that meant. The waiting was starting to get to me, and even though we'd only been gone a few days, I was already starting to feel like we were running out of time. Two weeks didn't seem long enough, but it was all we had, and while it had probably been a little naïve to think there would be an easy answer at Saylor's, I *had* hoped for . . . well, *something.*

Across the table, Blythe made a little sound of frustration, and I looked over at her. "What?"

She shook her head, dark hair brushing her shoulders. "I don't know what Dante took out of this book," she said. "But whatever it was, it was big. Saylor has all these notes about trying 'something' and reading about 'the spell,' but she never says what it *is.* And then right before the ripped pages, she's all excited and saying that if this works, it'll change everything and then . . ."

Blythe lifted the journal, letting it fall open wide so that the jagged edges of paper stood up slightly. "I always hated that dude," she said with a sigh.

Frustrated, I snapped another chip in half, the sound of mariachi music seeming louder and more annoying now. "Okay, so as soon as Saylor dies, Alexander sends his lackey to find Saylor's journal, but Dante doesn't take the whole thing, just rips out the pages he needs. Why? It would've been easier just to take the book."

"If someone took the whole book, Saylor would've known," Blythe said, shrugging. "But ripping out a few pages wouldn't have set off the magical alarm, as it were." She frowned. "Which is weird, actually. Most of the spell stuff I've found of hers was a lot more careful and well-done. But the magical alarm she put on this thing? That was done in a hurry."

I nodded, but thinking about that—Saylor knowing that once she took David, she could never go back home again, and doing a quick spell on her journal, thinking she was leaving it somewhere safe—just made me feel sad all over again.

"You know what?" I said, sliding out of the booth. "I'm not all that hungry."

I wasn't surprised that Bee followed me out of the restaurant, and when we stood in the parking lot, she looked over at me. Well, down at me. Bee really was freakishly tall.

"So I'm not sure if you know this," she said, "but Blythe kind of sucks."

I crossed my arms. "She's not my favorite person, I'll admit, but . . . I don't know. She hasn't been as bad as I thought."

Bee shaded her eyes from the sun with one hand, squinting at me. "If you say so. You know, we could ditch her," she suggested, and I wasn't totally sure she was joking. "Let her find her own way back to wherever she came from."

Not gonna lie, the idea was tempting, but I thought of that book—all its secrets and weird spells or whatever—and knew that Blythe was still our best chance of fixing David. And with my powers out of whack, we needed all the help we could get. "No," I said to Bee now. "Although I reserve the right to abandon her at a rest stop if she tries to shush me again."

Bee laughed at that and wrapped an arm around my shoulders, tugging me close. "Deal." She gave me another quick squeeze before stepping back. "I swear, she's lucky my Paladin powers are fading because the 'shh' thing definitely made me feel punchy."

Bee's voice was light and she was still smiling, but I noticed the way she didn't quite meet my eyes when she said it, and I touched her arm.

"Are you bummed?" I asked her. "About your powers going away?"

Bee shook her head, but she wasn't smiling anymore. "Not . . . bummed, exactly? It was just that I'd kind of gotten used to them, I guess, and the idea of being, I don't know, *normal* again while you and Ryan are still superheroes—"

"My powers are on the fritz, too," I reminded her. "And who knows what will happen with Ryan."

Bee looked over at me, her fingers tugging at the hem of her T-shirt. "You fought that girl at the motel," she reminded me. "I didn't see it, but it sounds like your powers were fine then."

Now it was my turn to shake my head. "It's not like I'm getting weaker, it's just that they keep . . . flickering on and off? Like a faulty switch or something."

That was the best way I could explain it. Honestly, I think it would've been a relief if they had just been getting weaker. Not knowing if I'd suddenly lose all my strength? That was the scary part.

I was going to say that to Bee, but she just lifted her head, glancing around. "You wanna walk for a bit, see what's what?"

So that was clearly the end of *that* talk. I nodded, needing both the space from Blythe and some fresh air.

We set off down the sidewalk. In a lot of ways, this little town was basically like Pine Grove. Well, like Pine Grove if people like my aunts and Saylor Stark hadn't tried to take care of it. You got the sense that it had been pretty once, quaint and charming, all of that. But the big terra-cotta planters outside the shops were filled with dying flowers, and, perhaps most tragically of all, there were still Christmas decorations hanging up on the streetlights. I stared at a faded green tinsel tree for a long time, taking deep breaths and trying not to panic. For the first time, I actually felt far from home, and even though Bee and Blythe were with me, I felt lonely.

Scared.

In that moment, I would've given most anything to be able to get back in the car and drive all night to get to Pine Grove. To sleep in my own bed underneath my white-and-purple comforter and wake up in the morning to my mom burning bacon.

I thought back to Saylor's brother, and the sad, faded air of the town took on new significance. Had Saylor longed for this place like I longed for home now? Had she looked at the streets of Pine Grove and thought of another small southern town? It had been Saylor's idea to put those big terra-cotta planters outside Magnolia House. After finding out that she was a Mage, I'd assumed everything she'd done as part of the Pine Grove Betterment Society had been about putting up wards, making the town safe for David. But maybe she'd really done some of those things just to make Pine Grove . . . better.

More like home.

My eyes stung all of a sudden, and I could feel a lump welling up in my throat. Saylor's death had hit us all hard, but it was almost like we'd all worked so hard to put it behind us that we'd never taken any time to mourn her. Standing in the streets of her hometown now, I missed her more than I had since she'd died, I think. I'd looked at Saylor for so long as the Woman Who Knew Everything. Even before all the Paladin stuff, she'd been my role model, and now I understood that we were more alike than I'd ever guessed. I didn't just want her back to fix stuff for us or tell us what to do. I wanted her back so that we could talk about what she had been before. How she'd managed to choose her duties as a Mage over the life she'd led here in Ideal, Mississippi. If she'd ever regretted it.

"Hey," Bee said, pulling me out of my thoughts. "What's wrong?"

I really didn't want to be the weird girl crying in the middle of a town square, so I did my best to stop the tears before they could fall, but it was a losing battle. I was already sniffling, and with a disgusted sound, I scrubbed at my face. "We should've told him," I said. "Saylor's brother. Or *I* should've told him. I . . . I owed that to Saylor."

Bee frowned, folding her arms over her chest. "But then he'd know she was dead. He'd have questions, Harper. How she died, where she's buried, why no one called the police . . ."

Sighing, I rubbed the back of my neck. "I know, but it feels wrong. To keep lying like this, to always be covering stuff up or wondering how to get away with things. I'm just . . ." Trailing off, I took another deep breath. "I'm tired of it."

She was right, obviously. Telling Saylor's brother that she'd died would open up a whole other can of worms, one I didn't have time for right now, but it was another reminder of just how badly magic could screw things up. Saylor had done a spell on her brother that would have him just kind of vaguely remembering her for the rest of his life.

Was it worth it, preserving all these secrets at a cost like that?

I was just about to turn and say so to Bee, but before I could, agony erupted in my head.

Crying out, I slammed my eyes shut against the sudden flare of light, my vision completely whiting out, my stomach rolling with the pain in my temples. I had the briefest moment of wondering if I was having a migraine, and then it was like the entire world dropped away. I wasn't on a street corner in Ideal anymore, surrounded by the heat of a southern summer. I was actually a little cold, standing in a dim space, the smell of moisture and earth all around me, a distant dripping sound in my ears.

A man stood in front of me. Well, a boy, really. Dark hair

curled over his ears, and he was wearing a dingy robe, the hem ragged and splattered with mud. His eyes were glowing so brightly that I fought the urge to cover my face against the glare.

We were in a cave, I realized, glancing up to see stalactites dripping from the ceiling, and even though some part of my mind knew I was still standing on the sidewalk in Ideal, there was nothing of that here. This was a vision, I knew it, but it definitely felt real.

The boy in front of me didn't react to me, all his concentration centered on a crack in the ground in front of him, wispy steam rising up. At his side, his dirty fingers opened and closed, opened and closed.

I'd seen David make that same gesture before when he was anxious, and something about it made my chest ache and my mouth go dry.

And then, just as quickly as it had come on, the vision was gone, and I was gasping on the sidewalk, leaning on one of those giant planters, sweat dripping down my face.

For one horrible second, I thought I was going to throw up right there in the middle of downtown, and I swallowed hard, sucking in a deep breath through my nose.

What the heck had *that* been? I knew it was a vision of some kind, that the boy I'd seen had been an Oracle. Had it been Alaric?

In my dreams, I'd seen a glimpse of someone who looked like him, and I knew that my dreams were somehow connected to David, but those had *felt* like dreams. Just hazy, distant things while I was sleeping.

This was like a full-scale hallucination while I was wide-awake, and it scared the heck out of me.

Suddenly I remembered Bee, and that she'd had just as many dreams of David as I had. If that was true, then shouldn't she—

Sure enough, when I lifted my head, I saw Bee leaning against a brick wall, her face pale, her hands on her thighs as she took deep breaths. Her blond hair was sweaty against her temples, and when her eyes met mine, I had my answer.

Whatever it was that had happened, it had happened to both of us.

Chapter 20

"TELL ME AGAIN."

I took another gulp of bottled water, closing my eyes for a second. We were sitting in my car in a parking lot at a local ball field, and the occasional *crack* of wooden bats against baseballs was making my head hurt even more than it already did.

"I've told you twice now," I said to Blythe, reaching out to turn the air-conditioning even higher, the cold air blowing my sweaty hair away from my face. Blythe frowned, closing the driver's side vents with more force than was necessary in my opinion, and from the backseat, Bee made a sound of protest. She was lying down back there, knees tucked up to her chest. Both of us were clearly worse for wear after . . . whatever had happened, and repeating the story to Blythe was exacerbating everything.

But Blythe was nothing if not determined, and she kept looking at me until I tipped my head back against the seat and, in a dull voice, repeated everything I'd seen. The dark-haired boy with the glowing eyes, the cave, the wispy vapor snaking up from the cracked earth . . .

When I was finished, Blythe's frown only deepened, and she reached down for the bag at her feet, rummaging through it.

"So you were dreaming about David or seeing whatever he's been seeing in visions," she confirmed, and I gave a weak nod.

"And now," she continued, "you're having full-on visions in the middle of the day. Both of you."

"Seems to be the case," Bee offered, sitting up. She was still a little pale, and she'd drained one bottle of water already, another half empty in her hands.

Retrieving Saylor's journal, Blythe flipped through it while I stared listlessly through the chain-link fence in front of us. A kid around our age was running bases, his dark blond hair shaggy underneath a cap.

"Why did you bring us here?" I asked. Blythe had found both of us standing on the street, shaky and rattled, and for the first time on this trip, I'd gratefully turned my keys over to her. She'd driven unerringly to this field before putting the car in park and demanding to know what happened. She'd asked on the street, too, but Bee and I had both been too wiped to get into it there.

Now she looked up briefly, watching that boy jog past us. "Cute boys," she said, as though that were explanation enough.

"Eye candy helps you think?" Bee asked, sounding a little more like herself, and Blythe gave a little shrug.

"Doesn't hurt."

It was hard to argue with that, and I sipped more water, taking deep breaths and waiting for the weight in my chest to lessen. It didn't, though, no matter how many baseball players I attempted to ogle.

Seeing what David was seeing, sharing a vision with him . . . was that something good or something bad? Did it mean we were getting closer to him, or that he was getting worse?

Or both?

Next to me, Blythe made a sound of surprise, her finger stabbing at one of the pages. "Okay, here we go. So when Alaric super-Oracled out, the Paladins couldn't find him for days."

I looked over at the page she was reading from, but it was just another mess of Greek and symbols with the occasional English word thrown in. Not for the first time, it occurred to me that we were having to trust Blythe a lot on this thing. We were trusting that her magic could fix this, *and* we were assuming she was telling the truth about whatever it was she was finding in Saylor's journal.

I wasn't sure how to feel about that.

For now, though, I just leaned closer, encouraging her to go on. "Turned out he'd hidden himself away in some cave for days, sort of . . ." Blythe lifted her head, nose wrinkling. "Leveling up, I guess. Concentrating his powers, getting ready for what was coming next."

I didn't like the sound of that and shifted uncomfortably in my seat.

"What does that mean?" Bee asked, leaning forward slightly.

"Well, we know he killed most of the Paladins, for one," Blythe said, and turned her attention back to the journal, one chipped pink nail skating underneath the words and symbols there. "But before he did that, he went back to his hometown, Aruza. And he—"

Her words died abruptly, and Blythe's finger slid from the page.

"What?" I asked, and she looked over at me, her dark eyes unreadable. "He, um. He blew it up, basically. Mages had put symbols all over the town to keep him safe there, and I guess after he escaped, he felt like those symbols might be used to hold him back or something." She shrugged, narrow shoulder moving underneath the bright pink and white stripes of her sundress. "Or maybe he was just really pissed they'd put them up in the first place."

I'd thought that sick feeling was fading away, but now I stared at Blythe, my palms suddenly sweaty on the water bottle. "So what, you think David's seeing Alaric when he went crazy?"

"I think there's a good chance, yeah," she said, closing Saylor's journal. I noticed the way her fingers curled around the book, and thought she might not even realize she was doing that. "Like I said, I don't know anything about Paladin stuff, but if you're both having daytime visions now, *and* you're both seeing what he's seeing, we could be close. That has to be what that means, right?"

She looked at both me and Bee, and I didn't know what to tell her. She was bringing the Mage knowledge on this trip, and if we were supposed to bring the Paladin knowledge, we weren't doing the best job.

But I sat up straighter in my seat, twisting the cap back onto my water bottle. "That has to be what it means," I said. "And maybe it's a clue, too. If he's seeing Alaric when he went nuts, he could be following the same path."

The more I said, the more excited and energized I suddenly felt, and I fumbled with my seat belt, already waving at Blythe to get out of the car and switch places with me. "So he might be heading for a cave, and there are tons of caves in the South. We'll look at a—I don't know—a guidebook or something. Check out Google."

"We have to find him before he gets there, though," Blythe said. "Once he's at the cave and doing whatever it is that makes him all super Oracle, it'll be too late."

That made my stomach hurt a little, but I waved it off, still going. "If Bee and I are connected to him, we might be able to sense which one it is, and then there he'll be, and—"

But Blythe wasn't moving and just watched me, still scowling slightly.

"And what are we going to do if we find him?" she asked, then shook her head. "No, we have to get the *spell* first. Whatever it was Dante took out of this." She shook the journal at me. "Once we have that, we can use the visions and your connection to David to find him."

I froze, my hand still on the door handle. "But . . . we could find him without all that," I said, my skin feeling itchy with the desire to move. "We've only been after him for two days, and we could already be *there*." Between the vision and that strange, almost-tugging sensation in my chest, I knew that David wasn't that far away, and when I looked back to Bee, she nodded, confirming that she felt him nearby, too.

"And without the spell, all that will happen is he'll blast us into the next century," Blythe argued. "Maybe literally for all we know. There's no telling what a rogue Oracle is capable of. I get that you want to find him, but we need the magic to *fix* him first. No." She shook her head again. "Our best plan is to find Dante and that spell. And what Alexander wanted with it," she added, almost to herself, and my frustration nearly had me shouting.

"Who cares what Alexander wanted with it? He's *dead,* and it doesn't matter. What matters is that we finally have a way to track David and get to him and—"

"And?" Blythe echoed, raising her eyebrows. "Seriously, Harper, what are you going to do if you find him?"

When I didn't have an immediate answer, she pointed a finger at me. "Without magic, all we have is your Paladin power, but that's kind of useless against him, isn't it? You can't hurt him, so what's the point of you charging in after him if you can't use magic *and* you can't kill him?"

Bee was watching me but she didn't say anything.

Killing David had always been there, a dark whisper in the back of my mind. Saylor had warned me that I might have to one day, and David had seen me driving a sword through him. I'd seen myself killing him in one of the trials Alexander had set up last year. But that didn't mean I was willing to accept it was an actual option.

But Blythe had a point—no spell, no plan.

Closing my eyes, I sagged back against the seat. "Dammit," I muttered, and Bee sighed.

I wondered if it was with relief.

But then I opened my eyes and looked at Blythe, pointing at

her. "But no more than two days," I told her. "We can't let him get too far away, and we're running out of time."

Two weeks was all we'd given ourselves for this, and we were already two days in. Twelve days just didn't seem nearly long enough to find Dante, get the spell back from wherever it was, and track David before he'd gone too far.

But, I reminded myself, I'd done lots of impossible things before. No one had thought we could afford five school dances in one year, and hadn't I found the funds? And that time we'd competed in the state cheerleading competition despite having a squad of only six people? Sure, we hadn't *won,* but we hadn't come in *last,* either.

We could do this.

Blythe smiled at me then, finally opening the driver's side door. "I can do it in one, promise," she said, and I got out of the car, hoping yet again that she was actually telling the truth.

He wasn't sure he was ever awake anymore.

Or maybe he never slept. It was getting harder and harder to tell the difference between sleeping and waking because the visions never stopped. Once, he thought, there had been a time when he could have shut the visions out, or at least waited for them to pass. Once, he thought, someone had set up wards to protect him from having visions. That had made him angry, but now as he lay in the darkness, his head splitting all the time, he understood that whoever that was had maybe been right.

That was another thing, the way names had slipped out of

his mind. Sometimes he imagined that it wasn't light pouring out of his eyes, but memories. Like he was leaking knowledge or losing . . . something. Maybe losing who he used to be.

But that was a crazy way to think. There was still enough of him inside his mind to know that. To know that something was wrong, that he was changing into something bad. But what? And how could he stop it?

Groaning, he rolled over. He thought he'd shut his eyes, but couldn't tell. After the last girl, he'd known he couldn't be around people anymore. It wasn't safe. So he found a perfect spot to hide. But now he couldn't remember how he'd found it or how he'd even gotten here. He was forgetting everything except the things he saw all the time. Blood on a yellow dress. A girl with green eyes, tears. Two other girls, but they couldn't help. And that was good.

The girl with the green eyes was dangerous. She was coming for him, and he could feel her drawing closer. The girl with the green eyes made something ache inside his chest, and he knew there was more he should remember about her. More he should *feel* about her besides how dangerous she was. But that was another thing he was losing, a fading memory that belonged to whoever—whatever—he was before.

And those things didn't matter anymore.

The girl with the green eyes wasn't going to stop coming, he knew that. He could hide, but she would find him because she wanted . . . something.

With a groan, he pressed his head to the hard rock beneath him, wishing the pain would stop, just for a little while. If the pain would go away, he could think. He could remember why the girl made his chest ache with something that wasn't just fear.

But the pain didn't stop, and the light was so bright, burning and illuminating the walls around him, and he thought maybe he screamed, but that sound could have just been in his mind. He didn't know anymore.

Still, lying there in the cold, damp dark, something came to him with a sharp clarity that burned everything else away. The yellow dress he kept seeing . . . was it hers? The girl's? And the blood that stained the front of it was his. There was a part of him that didn't feel bothered by that. A part that welcomed it. This wasn't a life, after all, so who cared if it ended?

But the other part of him fought against that. He was ancient and powerful, not something that should be put down like a feral dog. He was the Oracle, and this girl, this Paladin, wanted to stop him. She would kill him.

Unless he killed her first.

Chapter 21

"No."

"Yes."

"Except no."

I sat in the driver's seat, staring at the dive in front of me, my fingers tight around the steering wheel. At one point in its existence, the bar had maybe been called "Cowboys." I was guessing this based on the cardboard cutout of a cowboy propped up near the door, and the fact that there was a sign on the roof that had an "O," a "W," and a "Y" on it. Other letters had fallen off or rotted away.

In short, it was clearly the worst place in the world, and I could not believe I was going to have to set foot in there.

Blythe was in the passenger seat, eyebrows raised as she looked over at me. "I'm telling you, this is where he is."

From the backseat, Bee snorted. Her hair was loose tonight, and she pushed it back with impatient hands. "Why would anyone want to hang out here?" she asked. "This is a place where you end up on a true-crime TV show."

Truer words had never been spoken, but Blythe folded her arms over her chest, staring at the bar. "In any case, this is the place where he is."

Before we'd driven out of Ideal, Blythe had done a quick tracking spell on Dante. Apparently, his fingerprints on Saylor's journal had been enough, and after a brief ritual done in a Shell station bathroom, Blythe had come out with a location in mind.

Stupidly, I'd assumed we'd be heading to a house. Maybe an apartment. Not this truly sad dive bar in eastern Georgia.

We'd been driving for about five hours, and while the sun had just gone down, the parking lot was already packed, telling me that the clientele here at "OW Y" took that whole "five o'clock is drinking time" thing seriously.

I was not looking forward to a night sifting through the local drunks for one guy.

But if this was where Dante was, then this was where we had to be. Still, I had some reservations.

"We're teenagers," I reminded her now. "They won't let us in."

"We're *girls*," Blythe countered. "They'll let us in."

She probably had a point there, but I still wondered if maybe Bee and I should hang out in the car.

Leaning forward, Blythe continued. "Plus we have mind-controlling magic. Haven't y'all ever used the Mage's powers to get into bars?"

I looked over at her, scowling. "Um, no, we don't use the special superpowers Ryan got because Saylor *died* in order to score beer, actually."

But then Bee leaned in closer and said, a little sheepish, "One time, Ryan used it to get us into that new restaurant in Montgomery? The one it's hard to get reservations to?"

I turned in my seat, blinking at her, and she shrugged. "It was our one-month anniversary, and he wanted to take me somewhere special. It didn't *hurt* anyone."

Rolling my eyes, I turned back around to face Blythe's triumphant smile. "Okay," I said, taking the keys out of the ignition. "Fine. Let's go use the powers of the gods to dodge creepy guys and drink cheap beer and find this other guy who apparently holds the key to everything."

We stepped out of the car, gravel crunching under our feet. The door was open, and loud, raucous music was pouring out into the night. I could hear the stomping of feet on the wooden floors, and the smell of stale beer and fried food hung like a fog over the building.

I stood there at the base of the steps leading up into the bar as Bee and Blythe walked in front of me, heading on in. "Seriously, *why this place?*" I muttered, but Blythe didn't answer me. After a minute, I sighed and followed.

I wish I could say that "OW Y" was not what I expected and that I learned a valuable lesson about not making snap judgments, but no. No, I was totally right, and it was totally gross. The music was too loud, and despite the name of the bar—or what I was guessing was the name of the bar—I didn't see a single cowboy hat. I saw a *lot* of baseball caps, though, and more fraternity shirts that I could count, plus a fair amount of giant belt buckles.

"Wait at the bar!" Blythe shouted over the music (some ungodly bro-country song about trucks and rivers and girls in short shorts), and I caught her arm before she could disappear.

"Don't you need us?" I asked, and she shook me off with an irritated look.

"Let me find him first," she called out. "Better if I do that part on my own."

With that, she turned away and was promptly swallowed up by a wave of plaid and denim.

Sighing, I wove my way through the crowd, making my way to the bar. Not that I wanted a beer—ew—but I did want somewhere to sit and a bottle of water. This place was packed, and also hot as Satan's armpit.

There were two empty stools, and I propped my hip on one, leaning in to shout at the bartender. I'd just asked for the water when I sensed someone sliding onto the stool beside me, and without even bothering to look over, I held up one hand. "No. No to whatever you're about to say; go away, please."

A hand curled around mine, and I jerked my head around, prepared to send some redneck crashing through the opposite wall if I needed to, but it was just Bee, shaking her head and laughing at me.

"Easy there," she said. "I was coming to be your wingwoman."

Snorting, I took my bottle of water from the bartender, handing him a few crumpled dollars from my pocket. "Yeah, because picking up dudes is what I'm here for in *this* dump."

Bee nodded and glanced around. "You think this guy is actually here?"

Shrugging, I unscrewed the lid on my bottle. "Let's freaking hope so."

Bee had her hair in both hands, twisting it over her shoulder, and at that, she lifted her eyebrows. "I can't imagine she'd want to come here for fun, Harper."

I couldn't see Blythe in the press of bodies on the dance floor, so I had no idea where she was. Scowling slightly, I looked back to Bee. "No telling with her."

"That's the truth," Bee replied, before looking back at me with a slight lift of her eyebrows.

"Not used to taking the backseat, huh?"

The words were light and teasing, and they shouldn't have bugged me, but I found myself frowning and turning on my stool to face her better. "What?"

Clearly picking up on my tone, Bee gave an uneasy shrug. It was hot in the bar, and her hair was already curling in the humidity. "You're just used to being in charge is all. And now, because Blythe has the magic we need, we have to trail after her." Another lift of her shoulders. "It has to feel weird, is all."

It did, but I didn't really want to talk about that, not even with Bee. Especially since it made me wonder if this was what *she* had felt earlier in the year, me always trying to decide what was best, plowing on without actually asking anyone else how *they* felt about it.

I'd made her and Ryan ride shotgun—sometimes literally, but mostly metaphorically—a lot. Riding shotgun wasn't a great feeling.

I smiled at Bee and tried to keep my tone light. "Not so weird. I'm just annoyed that we're spending time in a dump like this."

Leaning back on her stool, Bee fished in her pocket for her phone, pulling it out to take a picture of the stuffed dance floor. "For Ryan," she told me, and I nodded and smiled and missed David.

I fumbled for my own phone, pulling it out of my pocket and scrolling through the picture gallery. There were lots of pictures of David. Him on the computer in the newspaper lab. Him grimacing as he held up one of the huge construction-paper daisies I'd made for the Spring Fling dance.

One of him sitting underneath a tree in the courtyard at the Grove, smiling at me. His hair was a wreck because of course it was, but the pale green shirt he was wearing made his eyes look especially blue, and the sunlight lined him in gold. Not from any magic, no crazy Oracle powers spilling out of him. Just a cute boy, smiling at me because he liked me.

My throat felt tight, and even though I knew it was stupid and pointless, I took a quick snap of the scene around me. The dudes in trucker hats, the girls in really short shorts, the general "this is where you come not only to drown your sorrows, but also to obliterate your brain" vibe.

The flash made the whole thing look even more depressing, but it made me smile a little anyway as I texted it to David's number, a number I knew wasn't working anymore.

Wish you were here, I typed, and then, before I could let myself think, I hit send.

There wasn't any reply; I hadn't expected there to be. But I still watched my phone for a long time.

"Hey, pretty lady," a voice slurred, and the stool on the opposite side of me jostled slightly.

I didn't bother looking up. "No," I said, raising one hand, eyes still trained on my phone.

A gust of boozy breath, and then a slurred "I ain't even asked you a question yet!"

"No," I repeated, keeping my hand up, and after a moment, there was another huff of breath, and then he was gone, lumbering off to find some other girl.

I looked up at Bee, then, but she was still grinning down at her phone, clearly texting with Ryan.

Sighing and feeling way more sorry for myself than was attractive, I stood up, determined to find Blythe. If she hadn't already found Dante, I was willing to give her about ten more minutes in this place.

I gingerly made my way around the dance floor, trying to keep my toes un-stomped while scanning for Blythe. This was where being short was a real pain in the butt, because I could barely see anything, and I was searching for someone even littler than I was.

I completed a full circuit of the floor and didn't see Blythe.

This was not only a giant waste of time, but also completely gross, and if there are any two things I hate in this world, it's wheel-spinning and nasty bars.

My hands felt gritty from just touching the chairs in this

place, so I made my way to the ladies' room—sorry, the "Cowgirls' Room" according to the sign—determined to wash up before enlisting Bee in my search for Blythe.

But when I opened the door to the bathroom, Blythe was already in there, standing by the sinks, fists clenched at her sides.

And at her feet was a guy, blood slowly trickling from his temple.

Chapter 22

"OH MY GOD, are you okay?" I asked, stepping over the guy's prostrate form to go to Blythe. She was breathing heavy and some of the hair had come out of her ponytail, but other than that, she seemed all right.

"Good!" she said, almost chipper, and held up a can of hair spray. "Stole this out of your bag and put it in my purse, hope you don't mind."

I looked at the bit of blood clinging to the bottom of the can and swallowed hard. I couldn't fault a girl for improvising a weapon, but now that can of Big Sexy Hair was headed for the nearest garbage can.

"If he touched you, I hope you at least gave him a concussion," I said, kicking at the bottom of the guy's shoe with my toes. "Now can we *please*—"

And then I looked closer at the guy on the floor.

Tall, Asian, definitely handsome despite the blood dripping from his temple . . .

"Dante?" I asked, and Blythe nodded, tossing the hair spray can in the trash.

"Yup. So no worries about me being okay. I knocked him out in the hall and dragged him in here."

I stared at her for a second, then looked back to Dante, who was starting to moan and move around a bit. "And the purpose of knocking him out was . . . ?"

Blythe put her hands on her hips. "I told you I always hated that dude."

Taking a deep breath through my nose, I studied my reflection in the grimy mirrors over the sink, telling myself I'd count to ten before I said something I regretted. "We have to ask him all kinds of questions," I said, keeping my voice steady, "so maybe giving him a concussion was a less-than-stellar plan?"

Dante moaned again, and I added, "And also, would've been nice to hear you'd found him before you clocked him."

Blythe tugged at the hem of her shirt, sniffing. "Fine. I just . . . I have trouble not leading, I guess."

That cut close to home. I nodded, then turned back to the guy on the floor.

Dante was conscious again, staring at both of us, befuddled. Whether that was because he'd been listening to us or from the damage Blythe had done with that can of Big Sexy Hair, I couldn't say.

"Ugh, finally," Blythe said, stepping over to Dante. "I didn't hit you *that* hard."

"Why did you hit me at all?" he said, hand still to his head. Then he glanced back and forth between us, wary.

"You're not, like, going to steal my kidney or something, are you? I saw that kind of thing on the news once."

Rolling her eyes, Blythe crossed her arms and cocked one knee. "Oh my God, Dante, don't act like you don't know me."

His eyes traveled over her, and if he was acting, he was doing a damn good job of it because he genuinely looked confused and scared. "I . . . don't?" And then he scowled. "Other than as the crazy bitch who hit me with . . . was that hair spray?"

Blythe dropped her arms and moved closer to Dante. "What are you talking about? Of course you know me. We worked together for over a year. We . . ." She glanced over at me, and then dropped her voice. "We made out that one time? At the office?"

The word "office" surprised me. It was so . . . normal. Did the Ephors have a regular building somewhere with, like, cubicles and fax machines? That was almost too bizarre to contemplate. As was the idea of Blythe making out with anyone. She seemed so . . . okay, no-nonsense isn't right, because Lord knew there was plenty of nonsense around Blythe, but she was . . . determined. Serious. She might have taken us to the ball field to ogle boys, but I hadn't actually seen her doing any ogling. I wasn't sure Blythe even liked boys. Or girls, for that matter.

Still, the idea that the same kind of drama that had been dogging me, David, Ryan, and Bee was *also* an issue for the Ephors was kind of funny, I had to admit.

This is what happens when you use teenagers for all your crazy world-controlling stuff, I thought.

But Dante was still watching Blythe, now less scared, more pissed off. "Look, I don't know you," he said, rising— more than a little wobbly—to his feet. "And if you hit me because you thought I was your ex or something, I feel really sorry for whoever it is you think I am."

Blythe stepped right up to him, rising on tiptoes to look at his face, and Dante flinched (not that I could blame him).

"You . . . seriously don't remember?" she asked, and he stepped back, one hand raised defensively toward his head.

"I'm telling you, I don't *know* you." He looked over to me. "Either of you."

"Blythe," I said, "I think he's telling—"

"The truth," she finished. "Yeah, me, too."

Someone rattled the bathroom door handle, and I was glad I'd had the presence of mind to lock it. But still, we were going to have to move fast now.

"Mind wipe?" I asked and she nodded slowly, still staring at Dante's face.

"Yeah, but . . . more than that, I think."

Without warning, she lifted her hand, and a bolt of . . . *something* shot out of it, smacking Dante firmly in the chest and making him yelp as he stumbled back against the toilet stalls.

"The hell?" he gasped, and I was thinking something similar.

But Blythe shook her head. "Mind wipe or no, he'd still have his powers," she said to me, even as Dante's eyes went wide.

"What?" he asked, but she waved him off.

"It's instinctual. He would have felt me charging up for that hit."

"I didn't feel you charging up for that hit," I countered, and Dante slumped against graffiti reading, "ASHLEY <3s BO."

"What are you talking about?" he asked. "What hit, what powers, wh—"

"Shut. Up," Blythe said in clipped tones, never looking over at him.

"Maybe he forgot he could do magic?" I suggested. "And that's the issue?"

But Blythe shook her head again. "No, that's what you're not getting here, Harper. It wouldn't matter if he *forgot* he could do magic; he'd still be able to do magic."

"But he can't," I said, looking back over at Dante, who was now pulling out his phone with trembling hands.

As he lifted it, Blythe reached over, smacking the phone from his hands, and he made a sound really close to a whimper. "You are not taking a picture of us, and we are not here to tell you you're going to be a superhero," she said. "You used to be, kind of, but clearly something got to you."

"Alexander?" I suggested, and Blythe nodded, watching as Dante scrambled for his phone.

"I'm guessing so, yeah."

"Which means . . ."

Heaving out a long breath, Blythe walked over to the bathroom door, unlocking it and letting Dante rush out of there. He nearly plowed right into Bee, who, it turned out, was the door rattler.

"What's going on?" she asked, watching as Dante bolted into the crowd.

Hands on her hips, Blythe sighed as he took off, and then turned to me and Bee, her eyebrows raised. "Well?" she said, nodding after Dante. "Go get him."

Chapter 23

THERE'S NO NEED in getting into what happened at "OW Y" after that. You really don't need to hear about me and Bee chasing the dude through the crowd, or how I maybe tackled him right by the jukebox, regretting my decision to wear a skirt that night. And you certainly don't need to hear about the various things the crowd shouted out, or how Bee and I ended up wrestling him out of the bar to cheers and clapping, and that before we got him in the car, I saw the flash of several phone cameras, and heard the words "Facebook" and "Twitter."

The main thing is that we got Dante out of "OW Y" and into a field just on the outskirts of town. And to be honest, standing in tall grass with Dante sitting in front of us, squinting against my headlights—I'd left them on to illuminate whatever it was Blythe wanted to do—I thought of those tawdry true-crime books Aunt Martha always got at Walmart. Back at the bar, I'd been afraid of being a victim in a book like that.

Staring at Dante now, I kind of felt like I might actually be one of the bad guys in that kind of book.

Not that we'd hurt him or anything. Other than a little cut

above his eyebrow where he'd hit it on the corner of the jukebox as he'd fallen, he wasn't hurt, and he seemed to be more angry than scared.

"You're totally going to cut out my kidney, aren't you?" he asked, and I tried to look both intimidating and nonthreatening, crossing my arms over my chest while still giving a reassuring smile.

As a result, I probably just looked confused when I said, "We don't want your kidney, trust."

He glared up at me, his dark hair falling over his forehead. Even pissed off and freaked out, he was pretty cute, so if he and Blythe *had* had something going on, I definitely couldn't blame her.

"Then what—" Dante started, but Blythe was already walking forward, Saylor's journal open in her hands, the headlights lining her in a bright white glow.

"There's nothing in here for reversing a spell this big," she said, ignoring Dante, who sat with his hands fastened behind his back with some of the spare bungee cords I'd brought in case we needed to strap luggage to the roof of my car.

"But," Blythe went on, her eyes moving over the pages, "I can try a . . . combination of things, maybe."

She sounded less than sure, but when she lifted her head, her expression was determined, her pointed chin thrust forward.

Bee and I had done our job as Paladins, using our strength to manhandle Dante into the car and out here, so now it was Blythe's turn to show what she could do.

The words that came out of her mouth made no sense to me.

I wasn't sure if they were Greek or just, you know, *magic,* but there was power in them, no matter how nonsensical they sounded. The hairs on my arms stood on end, and right next to me, I could feel Bee shiver.

Dante had gone still, his eyes so wide I could see the whites all the way around, and once again, an uncomfortable feeling slithered through me. I didn't like this, any of it, and whether the bigger problem was Blythe's magic or the kidnapping, I didn't know, but I definitely felt icked out.

But then Blythe stepped forward and stretched a hand out to me. "Come here."

I moved closer, putting my hand in hers. Her palm was clammy, making me wonder if she was a little creeped out by what we were doing, too.

Bee shuffled back a bit as Blythe and I approached Dante, and when Blythe pressed her fingers to his temples, she gestured at me to do the same.

I stood there, fingers out, but not touching him yet. "What are we doing?" I asked, scratching the back of my calf with the opposite foot. "Some kind of Vulcan mind-meld thing?"

David would've been proud of me for making that reference, but Blythe just glared. "We're seeing if getting inside his head will work," she said. "Whatever Alexander did to him, it wiped his memories and his powers. I want to know why and how, and I'm hoping the spell I just did will do that for us. Okay? Are we good now?"

"We're never good," I muttered, but it was more from habit than actual irritation.

When I pressed my fingers to Dante's temple, the only thing I felt was his damp skin, his sweaty hair against my knuckles, and I opened my mouth to tell Blythe that this was stupid, that it wasn't working.

And then it was like everything suddenly . . . tunneled. My vision went dim except for two pinpricks of light, like I was looking through a telescope the wrong way. It wasn't anything like the time I'd seen David's vision or even when Alexander had made me see things during the Periasmos last year. This was something new, something that had me feeling as though I were standing on very shaky ground, my knees wobbly, my heart racing.

For what felt like ages, there was just that sense of being in a dark tunnel and seeing those little bits of light. I could hear voices, but they were muffled—muted, like people talking in another room. I couldn't hear the sounds of the cicadas and frogs, couldn't feel the brush of the tall grass against my legs, or the suffocating warmth of a Georgia summer night anymore. It was like I wasn't *anywhere,* and even if I'd wanted to pull my hand back from Dante's temple, I don't think I could have.

And then suddenly, the tiny dots of light got bigger, rushing toward me. Or maybe I was rushing toward *them.* It was hard to tell. All I knew was that the darkness faded away, replaced by a scene that seemed awfully familiar.

Alexander, sitting behind his desk, his golden hair burnished in the lamplight. He was wearing a dark suit with a deep-green tie, looking exactly like he had every time I'd ever seen him, and as he rose from the desk, I realized that the office he was in was almost identical to the one he'd had in Pine Grove. That house had been magicked up, but it felt like what I was seeing was the real deal.

Because this was Dante's memory, we were seeing everything from his perspective. He was clearly sitting in front of the desk, wearing jeans, his fingers tapping nervously on one leg. Leaning back, his hands folded in front of him, Alexander looked anything but anxious. He was as calm and collected as I remember, and the smile he shot Dante was clearly meant to be welcoming. But I saw the edge to it and remembered that, too. For all his good manners and elegant style, Alexander had been dangerous, and Dante clearly understood that. I could see him jiggling one leg as he reached into the front pouch of his hoodie, pulling out ragged sheets of paper.

"Ah, very good," Alexander said, the words sounding slightly echoing and distorted, like he was talking underwater.

"It was easy to find," Dante said, lifting his chin a bit. "She'd set some kind of alarm spell on the book, but not on the pages themselves. Took me like ten seconds to find it and lift it."

"Sloppy," Alexander murmured, his eyes traveling over the page in front of him. "How unlike Saylor."

Feeling better now, Dante leaned back in his seat, crossing one ankle over the other. "That's some hard-core magic, though. Like, way outside my skill set. Probably outside Blythe's, even."

"Yes, well, it was always more theoretical than practical, this spell," Alexander said, but he didn't lift his eyes from the page, and I could swear his hand was trembling slightly.

"I'd hope so," Dante said, pushing his hood from his head.

"The power and memory wipe is one thing, but that last bit?" With a low whistle, he shook his head. "Man, that's *dark*. And intense. I wouldn't even want to try it. Be like that story, right? The one with the people who wish for—"

Alexander lifted a hand, cutting him off. "Like I said, the spell was theoretical. Something I asked Saylor to work on before she vanished so precipitously. I'd never meant to actually test it."

And then he suddenly smiled again, looking up at Dante and saying, "But no time like the present, hmm?"

He said some words then, nothing I understood, and the scene in front of me started to shake. I wasn't sure if the room itself had shaken when this happened, or if Dante's memories, locked away in some faraway corner of his mind, were just becoming unstable.

Either way, everything fell apart. There was a sound like wind wailing in my ears, and suddenly we were being thrust away again, hurtling backward, until I felt hot, muggy air again and the scratch of grass on my legs, and I was once again standing in a field, my hand falling away from Dante's head.

Next to me, Bee had a hand on my shoulder, her face creased with worry. "Are you all right?" she asked, and I nodded, even though I definitely wasn't sure about that.

I looked over to see if Blythe was all right, but her eyes were fixed on Dante, and when I turned my head, I saw why.

He was still staring sightlessly ahead, his chest rising and falling rapidly, but now a trickle of blood was slipping from his nose.

"What's going on?" I asked Blythe, and she shook her head frantically, paging through Saylor's journal.

"I . . . I think the spell was too strong. Or maybe Alexander added some kind of, I don't know, like, booby trap to it." Her voice was thin, higher than usual, and her fingers moved over the pages of the journal so quickly that death by paper cut seemed like a real hazard.

"You did a spell on him without knowing what it would do?" Bee asked, stepping forward and slightly out of the headlights' glare. She'd pulled her hair into a messy bun, and she was looking at Blythe with her eyebrows raised. "Isn't that what you gave us so much crap for?"

Blythe's head shot up. "The kind of magic we're dealing with is *dangerous*," she spit out. "I'm sorry it's not a freaking chemistry problem with *formulas* or whatever, but it's not, and—"

"And the two of you need to stop fighting and figure out what we're going to do," I finished, crouching down at Dante's side. His pulse was strong underneath my fingers, even though he was still breathing fast. Still, in the bright glow of my headlights, his pupils were so wide that there was hardly any iris showing.

"Should we call nine-one-one?" I asked, wondering what we would even say to a dispatcher. "'Hi, we did magic on this guy in a field and now he seems catatonic, please assist'?"

But then Dante's head suddenly whipped in my direction, his hand flying out. The ground rumbled and a wave of power shot out from his fingertips, strong enough to knock me backward, making my teeth clack together hard.

"The hell?" Bee squawked, but I was already on my feet, reaching for Dante.

Another wave hit, no real specific spell, just magic, lots of it, powerful enough to make all the hair on my arms stand up and to start a ringing in my ears.

"He's not supposed to have powers!" I yelled, but that seemed kind of ridiculous to say when he lifted his hand again, sending out another bolt that had Bee stumbling against the hood of the car.

Blythe was still looking through the journal even as she had one hand out, sending blasts of power. But they just seemed to roll off Dante, who was already rising to his feet and raising his hand again.

Blythe cried out as the journal flew from her hands, and I was so freaked out from taking a walk through Dante's mind that I wasn't sure if my powers were up to the challenge of taking on a Mage Gone Wild.

But I was certainly willing to give it a shot.

As I moved forward, something caught my elbow, and I turned to see Bee next to me. Apparently her stumble against the car had given her an idea.

When I got my first car, my dad had given me a toolbox for the trunk. It was pink (and both the hammer and the screwdriver inside had flowers on their handles), which I'd appreciated, but it was also heavy as all get out. As she held it out to me, and as I closed my fingers around the handle, I flashed Bee a smile. "Thanks, Squire."

"Thought there might be something in there that would help!" she said quickly, already moving back.

And maybe there was, but then Dante was turning his gaze back to me, and I realized I wasn't going to have time to rifle through the box for the handiest tool.

Instead, I hefted the entire thing, power flowing through my muscles, and swung.

Hard.

Chapter 24

"I MEAN, AT *most*, there's, like, a thirty percent chance I killed him."

We were speeding down the interstate toward Atlanta, the car thick with tension. I'd let Bee drive, and now I twisted from my spot in the passenger seat to look at Blythe in the back.

"He was out when we left, but he was still breathing. And we called nine-one-one. I'm sure he's fine."

I really hoped he was fine. Aunt Jewel had had a hard enough time with the break-in at David's. On the run for murder? I wasn't sure she could forgive that.

Blythe sank back farther into her seat. "He'll be fine," she agreed, her voice dull. "His magic would've acted kind of like a buffer. You knocked him out, but that was about all the damage you could do. And you were only able to hurt him because you're a Paladin."

"Good to know," I said, turning back around.

Silence fell again.

It wasn't broken until Bee flipped the turn signal at our exit, and against the steady *tick-tick* of that, she finally asked, "So . . . what happened back there?"

I could hear rustling from the backseat as Blythe fidgeted around. "Spell got out of hand. I told you, magic's not something that's easy to control or predict. When I tried to unlock his memories, I . . . I must've unlocked his powers, too, but they were all out of whack and stuff."

"Understatement," I muttered, rubbing at the new scrape on my knee from where Dante had pushed me backward.

I tried to meet Blythe's eyes in the rearview mirror, but she was gazing at her lap, her expression troubled. Blythe wasn't used to failing, and while we'd gotten the information we needed— Alexander had Saylor's spell, a spell that could wipe power *and* memories, and the pages were probably in his office—the night still felt like a loss.

"It's fine," I said to Blythe now. "You couldn't have known that would happen, and hey! Now we're *that much* closer to the spell we need, which means *that much* closer to stopping David."

Blythe nodded, but didn't say anything, and after a while, I turned my eyes back to the dark roads in front of us.

If Saylor's house hadn't been what I expected, Alexander's office was actually much more in line with what I'd pictured—a high-rise that glittered in the darkness, its hundreds of windows reflecting the moon and streetlights.

Still, there was a weird feeling around the building as I parked the car in the attached deck. It felt . . . abandoned. Empty. And while I wasn't surprised there weren't other cars in the lot at this time of night—it was nearly three a.m.—I'd still thought there would be some janitors, a few lights on. *Something.*

Everything was still and quiet as we followed Blythe across the parking lot to the front doors. They weren't locked—or else they just opened for Blythe—and we walked into a large lobby that was mostly empty.

"Is this place magicked or just abandoned?" I asked, and she looked over her shoulder at me as we moved toward the elevator.

"Six of one, half dozen of the other. There was magic over it to keep people out, but once the person who did the magic died, it started falling apart pretty quickly. Locals think it's just an abandoned high-rise."

"And you're sure this isn't going to get us arrested?" Bee asked once the elevator doors were closed.

Blythe shook her head, drumming her fingers on the steel rail behind her, and Bee and I met each other's eyes behind her back. Whatever happened with Dante was still clearly weighing on Blythe's mind.

The doors opened, and the three of us stepped out into a deserted lobby, where there was an empty desk and a few chairs. The carpet underfoot felt almost damp, and there was a musty, unused smell to the place.

For a moment, Blythe stood there, looking around. And then she said, "It looks different."

"When was the last time you were here?" I asked, and Blythe frowned. All three of us had changed in a rest-stop bathroom on the way here. We'd chosen to wear black for this little expedition (which was maybe a little drama queen of us, but it had felt appropriate for sneaking into an abandoned high-rise), and

Blythe's hair swung over her bare shoulders, her skin pale against her dark tank top.

"A few years ago," she said. "When they interviewed me."

She didn't even bother whispering, so I didn't worry about keeping my footsteps quiet as we walked through the lobby, heading for a long hallway of doors. A few of them were open, but when I glanced inside, I didn't see anything. No desks, no chairs. Just plain, square rooms, some with a window, others completely dark.

We stopped in front of a closed door at the end of the hall. The doorknob turned in Blythe's hand, but the door stuck slightly in the jamb, and she applied her shoulder to it. "This is where I met Dante."

The door swung open, and I followed Blythe into the office, my heart thudding.

If the rest of the office had seemed generic, this one room was anything but. This was so clearly Alexander's space that I half expected to see him sitting behind the desk. The desk was the same heavy, wooden monstrosity he'd sat behind at the house outside of Pine Grove, and even the carpet on the floor looked the same, a pattern of heavy swirls on a crimson background.

It was clear no one had been in here in a while. Overhead was a broken skylight that had let in rain and leaves, and books had fallen off the tall bookcases, their pages warped with damp. How long had it been abandoned like this? And why had no one noticed?

"Told you things went to hell when Alexander died," Blythe said, shining the beam of her flashlight up.

"But you can't tell from the outside," I argued, and Blythe shrugged.

"Most of the magic went to hell. Not all of it."

Next to me, I could see the corners of Bee's mouth pulling down, and she wrapped her arms tightly around her body. "Is this where they brought you?" I asked her, keeping my voice low. It wasn't like I was afraid anyone would overhear. It was just that in this office, surrounded by Alexander's things, the sound of my voice was too loud in my ears.

Bee must have felt the same because she was basically whispering when she said, "I don't know. Maybe? It's . . ." Trailing off, she looked around. "It feels the same. I know that sounds dumb, but—"

"Not dumb," I assured her, grimacing as something crunched under my feet. Could've been broken glass, could've been some rodent's or bird's skeleton. I definitely wasn't going to try to find out.

"You don't remember because they mostly kept you in a kind of stasis," Blythe told us, her own footsteps crunching as she moved around the room. In the darkness, she was just a small, shadowy figure.

"Alexander didn't know what to do with you once I brought you back," she continued. "I thought he'd want proof that what I'd done had worked. I'd done the ritual, David was juiced up, *and* he could make Paladins. But instead, he was just mad I hadn't brought the Oracle back."

She turned to Bee then. "That's why your memories feel fuzzy.

You were kept upstairs"—she gestured with her flashlight—"for weeks before Alexander worked out that he might be able to use you to get to her." The beam of light swung in my direction now.

"The Oracle was always the only thing that mattered to Alexander," she said. "I was supposed to charge him up and then bring him back, and when I couldn't . . ."

The silence that followed those words was heavy. Finally, Blythe cleared her throat, turning away.

"Let's just say he didn't have any use for me after that." She kept moving around the office. Bee and I might have been freaked, but Blythe clearly did not share our hesitation. Flashlight bobbing, she scanned the shelves and heavy wood desk near the farthest wall. "If the spell is here, it'll be in this room," she said, her free hand smoothing back her hair. "This was it, the main place where he always was, doing . . . whatever. And he never liked me in here."

There was something about the way she said that that made me turn around and look at her. As always, she'd pulled her hair up in a high ponytail, and she had her free hand propped on her hip. She seemed determined and fierce, but underneath all of that was something else. It was almost like . . .

"Blythe, does this place scare you?" I asked, and she didn't look over at me. Instead, she took a deep breath through her nose, and for a long moment, I thought she wasn't going to answer me at all.

And then she walked closer to the big desk and said, "Nothing scares me."

She looked over at me, a dimple appearing in one cheek. It was a smile, but one I'd never seen from her before. Blythe's grins were usually of the "I am tiny and filled with magic and insane" variety, but this was almost rueful. "Still don't like this place, though," she added. "Can't you feel it?"

"It's a creepy abandoned building," I said, looking up and turning in a slow circle, taking in those endless ceilings and the jagged hole from the skylight. "All creepy abandoned buildings feel weird."

"This is a *special* one, though," Blythe said, walking around the desk to stare at the drawers. She reached for one, but it was clearly locked, and she rattled it harder, trying to break it by force before trying magic.

Or maybe she just felt like breaking something. I understood that.

I walked over, once again ignoring the little things going *crunch* underneath my tennis shoes, and nudged her aside. "This calls for my particular skill set," I told her. I curled my fingers around the drawer's knob, and when I yanked, the wood gave with a satisfying *crack*.

But the satisfaction was short-lived, since the drawer was empty. Or at least that's how it looked to me. But Blythe reached in anyway, waving her hands in the empty space, eyes closed. "Like I said, most of the magic around this place faded when Alexander died," she told me, "but there's still a little bit left. The really strong stuff hangs around even after the person who made it is gone."

We stood there in the silence while Blythe waved her hands around, and I tried not to feel too frustrated when once again, she pulled out a book.

Bee, however, clearly had no problem saying what was on her mind. "Oh, yay," she said, crossing one ankle in front of the other. "Another book probably filled with gibberish. Just what we need."

I probably should have tried to play peacekeeper, but sometimes the joy of having a best friend around is having her say the things you can't.

"Any sign of those sheets Dante tore out?" I asked.

But Blythe was already leafing through the book, her eyes roaming over the pages. Unlike Saylor's book, this one was in decent shape, a slim, black day-planner kind of thing that made my office-supply-loving heart sing.

"Seriously, Blythe, do you see—"

Blythe suddenly stopped on a page that was absolutely covered in writing, so dense that you could barely see the white of the paper for all the black ink. And then she offered me the book.

I took it, wondering if I'd even understand what it was that had her so freaked, or if it would just be more Mage Stuff.

But this time, the words scrawled over the page weren't indecipherable.

And they made my stomach drop to my knees.

Chapter 25

"So what does this even mean?" Bee asked, leaning over my arm, her eyes scanning the page.

"David's parents. The ones we've always wondered about?" I said, my heart practically in my mouth. "They weren't just normal people who had a magical baby. They were *Alexander* and the Oracle."

We all went quiet, lost in our thoughts. Maybe it didn't mean anything. Maybe an Oracle baby was just an Oracle baby, and coming from magical parents didn't necessarily make him special.

And then I read just a little bit further.

"Alaric," I said softly, and Blythe nodded, her expression grim while Bee raised her eyebrows at me.

"What about him?" she asked.

"He was another male Oracle born to an Oracle," I said, "and we know how he turned out."

Crazy, super-charged, murdering Paladins, and blowing an entire town off the map.

Bee was leaning so close to me that her hair brushed the back of my arm. "But it doesn't make any sense. If Alexander was David's father, why would he want him dead?"

But he hadn't wanted David dead. He'd wanted *me* dead so I'd be out of the way, allowing him to perform a ritual on David. A ritual that would make him more powerful and, he'd hoped, more stable. It had worked in one regard, and been an abysmal failure in the other. David became incredibly powerful, but the visions had still messed him up pretty badly.

When he'd skipped town, his powers had blown through all the wards Alexander had put up.

Wards that I now knew weren't necessarily about trapping David in Pine Grove, but protecting him.

I went back through all the time I'd spent with Alexander, trying to think of any moment I could remember when there was even the slightest hint that he cared about David. I remembered him talking to me about how getting personally attached to an Oracle would only hurt me, but had he really been talking about himself?

"Did you know this?" I asked Blythe now. "Or even suspect?"

Her face was pale in the dim light. "Suspected, yeah. Well, not *this* exactly, but that David meant more to him than just being his Oracle. There were only two people in the world who had a vested interest in David—besides you, Harper. And that was Saylor and Alexander."

She braced her hands on the desk, her eyes still on the book. "If anyone was trying to find a way to fix him—or to stop an Oracle gone rogue—it would be one of them."

"That's what that spell was about, then. Why Alexander wanted it."

She nodded and kept paging through the book, frowning.

"Alexander spent years researching what had happened to Alaric. The Ephors had tried to stop Alaric, had looked for ways of, I don't know, neutralizing him, I guess. Bringing him back from madness."

"Why bother?" Bee asked. She had stepped back a little, and I heard another crunch as she, too, stepped on either glass or something unmentionable. Seriously, the sooner we were out of this place, the better.

"Why not just kill him?"

For a second, I thought Bee was talking about David, and my head shot up.

"Alaric," Bee clarified. "If he was seeing things and making Paladins and sending them after the Ephors, why did they bother trying to save him?"

"Because they weren't monsters," Blythe said, not looking up from the book. "Maybe they wanted to find some way to help him instead of putting him down like a dog."

"It didn't work, though," I reminded her, that cold feeling still sitting at the base of my spine. "They did kill him."

Now Blythe lifted her head, her eyes meeting mine. "Because it was the last resort," she said. "It happens. Once he'd gotten to that cave and started powering up, there wasn't anything they could do *but* kill him."

I didn't like the way she said that but wasn't sure exactly how to reply.

And then Blythe looked down at the book and sucked in a breath.

There, at the end of the book, was a little paper pocket affixed to the back cover. It was probably just the slightly wavering beam of the flashlight that made it seem like Blythe's fingers were trembling as she pulled out two worn, folded sheets of paper.

When she unfolded them, gently smoothing the paper with her hands, I looked down, hoping I'd be able to understand what was written there.

This was another one of Saylor's weird ciphers, part Greek, part English, part symbols, and it all swam in front of my eyes.

Whatever was on those pages, though, Blythe got it. I actually watched her go pale, saw her eyes widen as she took it in.

"Well?" I asked, louder than I should have, but the suspense had me feeling like something was crawling all over my skin.

"It's definitely the spell," she said, and the paper crinkled as she lifted it, turning to look at the back. This time, there was no doubt her hands were shaking.

"Duh," I said, rolling my eyes. "Will it help? Can you do it?"

To my surprise, Blythe didn't look all that enthused. This was what she'd been looking for—what we'd brought her along for, after all—and instead of seeming pumped, she looked a little . . . sick, to be honest.

Frowning again, she turned back to the pages. "It's harder than I thought it would be," she said, and there it was again, that sinking feeling in the pit of my stomach.

"But you can do it," I pressed, and her head shot up, dark eyes meeting mine.

"You saw how things went with Dante. This kind of magic, it's . . . it's really complicated, Harper. It's unwieldy. This"—she rattled the papers at me—"won't just take David's powers, it'll wipe his mind, too."

I thought of Dante, sitting in that field, the confusion on his face. "Oh. Right. I . . . forgot that bit."

A David who was normal but didn't remember me? Or anything, for that matter? It was worth a shot, surely.

I thought about Bee, asking why they didn't just kill the Oracle when that was clearly the easiest course of action.

The idea of David looking at me blankly, no idea who I was . . . it sucked. It sucked a *lot*.

But it was better than the alternative.

"What about the other part?" I asked, and Blythe's head jerked up.

"What?"

"In the memory," I reminded her. "Dante said there was another part to that spell, some scary, intense thing he didn't think people should try."

Blythe glanced back at the paper. "Not sure," she said, then looked up, startled, as we heard a noise from outside.

The three of us froze. We heard footsteps, quick and soft, and saw a thin line of light underneath the closed office door.

Blythe turned off her own flashlight, plunging us into near darkness, and as quietly as she could, she slid the book from the desk, shoving it awkwardly in the waistband of her pants.

There was no sign that this was Paladin-related stuff, and we hadn't been attacked since that first night at the motel, but I was taking no chances. Wordlessly, I held my hand out, and Blythe put the flashlight in my open palm.

The three of us held very still, shrinking back into the shadows as I tried to think of what to do. Was it better to rush out, taking whoever it was out there by surprise, or should we wait, hoping they passed us by?

But then the door swung open, making the choice for me.

My fingers were tight around the handle of the flashlight, ready to swing.

A pair of teenagers came stumbling in, and I was about to leap at them when I realized they were giggling, arms looped around each other.

Not Paladins sent by David. Just . . . kids exploring a deserted building.

The guy was tall, his hair blonder and shaggier than David's, but there was still enough of a resemblance to make my stomach flutter. The girl in front of him was a little taller than me, but her hair seemed as dark in the dim light, and when she turned to face him, winding her arms around his neck, the gesture seemed familiar.

It was all still so mixed up for me—the Oracle, the boyfriend, the guy I'd known for so long—and I couldn't sort out how I felt about any of it. Stopping the Oracle might still mean losing David, and while this was still the best way, I wanted . . . something more.

Something easier.

I was so caught up in those thoughts that I didn't even notice Blythe until she was stepping slightly in front of me, hand raised, murmuring under her breath.

The couple stopped kissing. Or, rather, they froze, lips still touching, and Blythe gave a satisfied sigh. "Okay, that trick lasts like a minute," she whispered. "Let's go."

We hurried past the unmoving couple, making our way out into the silent hallway. Even before we got to the street, Blythe was already pulling the pages out of her waistband, and as soon as we were in the car, she was looking at them again.

"You can do it, right?" I asked, starting the car. Blythe had reached up, turning on the dome light overhead and making it slightly trickier to see the darkened streets in front of me.

For a long time, the only sound was Bee's breathing in the backseat and the rustle of the pages as Blythe read.

Then she lifted her head, looked at me, and said, "Well, if we're going to do this spell, we're going to need some supplies."

"So you *can* do it?" I asked, not taking my eyes off the road.

And when Blythe just made a sound low in her throat, I told myself that surely that was a yes.

Chapter 26

I DON'T KNOW if you've ever been to a flea market, but it's not exactly something I can recommend. I mean, unless you need some sketch jewelry, a puppy, or a cassette tape from 1988, flea markets usually don't have much to offer. But Blythe was sure that we could find what we needed for the spell at the one she'd seen advertised in one of those colorful flyers you can pick up outside a grocery store. After a less-than-comfortable night sleeping in the car, we pulled into the field serving as the parking lot and stared at all the booths laid out in front of us.

It was already hot: Sweat was beading on my upper lip (ew) and starting to trickle down my spine. The little colored triangular flags they'd hung up just lay there, limp and listless since there was no breeze. The air smelled of car exhaust, animals, and the faint tang of lemonade from a nearby concession stand. In a lot of ways, it reminded me of the Azalea Festival back home, just dingier and a little more depressing.

Which was quite the feat. Once you've watched grown men chase greased pigs, it's hard to find anything that actually seems scuzzier.

Bee slid the sunglasses up on her head.

"So whatever it is you need to do this spell, it's . . . here?"

Blythe nodded. Her dark hair was tucked behind her ears, and while she'd been quieter since our trip to Alexander's, she also seemed . . . more settled. Probably because we finally had a plan. I knew that was making *me* feel better, even as I tried to ignore the pang the thought of a memory-less David caused me.

Still, better that than a Super Oracle David or, even worse, a dead one, which was why I put up with this trip to the flea market to get whatever it was Blythe wanted.

"Where do we even start?" Bee asked, and Blythe looked around.

"Jewelry booths," she said, and gave a decisive nod. "Over there near the weapons stuff."

Which maybe seemed like a good idea, but this was a flea market, which meant that there were roughly nine thousand jewelry booths, and that wasn't even counting all the people advertising "rocks and gemstones." Blythe tackled one end of the long line of tables and open car trunks, and Bee and I headed for the other. I know we should have split up to save time, but I wanted to talk to Bee out of Blythe's earshot.

The table I picked was one of the nicer ones, spread with what was probably a Christmas tablecloth, bright poinsettias blooming across the white cotton. There were boxes of various polished stones—amethysts, fool's gold, plenty of quartz—and if what Blythe was after was in here, I sure couldn't feel it. Still, I poked through the rocks, and without looking over at Bee, said, "This is like trying to find a needle in a haystack. Or, you know, a magic rock in a box of not-magic rocks."

Bee snorted, her sunglasses back in place. "She said we'd be able to sense it if we touched it, right?"

I shrugged. "She did, but for all we know, that just means *she'll* be able to feel it. We could be duds at the Magic Rock Hunting Game."

"She was right about Alexander's place," Bee admitted, moving over to my table. Under the morning sun, her shoulders were tanned and freckled, and I wished I had thought of wearing a tank top. How could it be this hot when the sun had been up for only a few hours?

After nodding and smiling at the lady by my table, I strolled farther down the line, Bee trailing behind me. "She was," I said, passing a booth full of slightly grubby stuffed animals. "And I feel like she's right that we're on David's trail. It's just—"

"You're not crazy about this spell," Bee finished, and I stopped in front of another table of jewelry, rings and necklaces and stuff, all laid out on little velvet trays. I hated to keep groping people's wares without actually planning on buying anything, so I tried to run my finger over everything as quickly as possible before moving on, not lingering if I didn't have to.

"I'm really not," I told Bee. "I mean, I get it. If we can neutralize David, we keep him safe. We keep us and everyone we love safe. It's clearly the best solution."

"It is," Bee said, picking up a heavy turquoise stone on a silver chain, "but it's also a solution that ends with him not knowing who you are anymore."

There was no disagreeing with that. I'd told myself that I would do whatever it took to stop David *and* save him. That this was about me being a Paladin, not me being his girlfriend. But maybe that was just incipient heatstroke talking.

Speak of the devil, Blythe suddenly broke through the crowd, walking toward us, a little orange plastic bag dangling from one wrist.

As she approached, I could see that she was sweaty, too, her dark hair damp at her temples, her forehead glistening. "Okay," she said brightly, waggling an orange plastic bag at us.

"You found it?" I asked.

Eyebrows lifting over her sunglasses, Blythe stared at me. "No, I grabbed a cheap charm bracelet."

"Okay, okay, sarcasm earned on that one," I said. "So can we get out of here?"

And then she focused her gaze on me again.

"What about you?" she asked me. "Did you feel anything?"

Turning, I ran my hands over a box of rocks, but there was nothing, and I shook my head. "Nope."

Blythe frowned. "Nothing? No . . . pull to anything?"

I glanced back at her, and she was watching me in a way that made faint alarm bells go off in my head. "No," I repeated. "Which clearly we wouldn't have since *you* found whatever magic rock we need to do this thing."

"Did you try the table closest to the weapons display?" Blythe pressed, and confused, I started to shake my head.

And then my head was splitting open.

Or at least that's what it felt like.

But the agony was over quickly, and suddenly I was in a cave again, the damp, cool, earthy smell of underground surrounding me. This time, though, there was no hint of the sulfuric tang I'd picked up in the vision of Alaric.

And when I lifted my head, it wasn't him standing in front of me.

It was David, and he wasn't standing, but floating, the tips of his sneakers barely dragging against the rock. His chest was moving slowly, deep breaths that seemed to saw in my ears, breaths that I could feel in my own chest. The glow pouring from his eyes lit up his whole face.

In those moments, I felt like his breaths were mine, that our hearts were beating at the same time, and I could feel . . . anger. Hatred. Fear. His head was full of images: wards scratched into stone suddenly wavering into wards scratched into soft brick; people in robes milling around a dusty street suddenly becoming kids from Grove Academy. I recognized Ryan and Bee, saw the twins and Lucy McCarroll.

A beginning must end for a new beginning to start.

The words slid through my mind like smoke, and I could feel power in my—no, in David's hands as he clenched them into fists.

I came back to myself all at once, shaking and sick.

"Harper!" Bee cried, and I raised my head to look at her. She seemed worried, her mouth turned down at the corners, her gaze intent, but not freaked out. Not like me.

"What was it?" Blythe asked immediately, and I shook my head, unable to talk right away.

The sun suddenly seemed to be too hot, too bright, and I stumbled away from them, moving toward one of the big white tents set up along the flea's main thoroughfare. I pushed a flap away and moved inside, taking deep breaths, hoping I wasn't going to throw up all over someone's table of collectible shells.

But the tent was empty.

I stood there in the center of the tent, my breath rasping hard in my ears, trying to get my bearings and make sense of what had just happened.

"Harper," Bee said, coming in just behind me, "are you all right?"

It was obvious that I wasn't, but before I could say anything, the tent flap moved again. I was expecting Blythe, but instead, it was a taller girl with lighter hair, moving fast. She pushed Bee hard as she came in, and Bee immediately stumbled, falling to her knees with a soft cry.

And then the girl was on me.

Chapter 27

I FELL BACK, more from the surprise than anything else, but was able to recover fast enough, shooting to my feet and whirling around, not surprised at all to be confronted by another teenage girl.

Behind the girl, Bee was rising to her feet again, and I saw her hands flex at her sides, but she wasn't making any move to jump in. That told me all I needed to know about just how great Bee's powers were doing right now.

Sighing, I crouched a little, holding out my hands in front of me. This was the third girl I'd had to take on in a few days; while I'd managed okay with the other two, I wondered if there might be a better tack to try with this one. "What's your name?" I asked as we circled each other on the stamped-down grass underneath the tent. "I'm Harper Price."

"I know that," the girl all but snarled. Her hair was the kind of blond sometimes called—not very nicely in my opinion—"dishwater," and she was wearing a T-shirt with some boy band on it. I looked at all their disturbingly smooth-skinned faces, and really hoped I won this fight.

Getting my butt handed to me by a girl wearing that shirt was too humiliating to contemplate.

"We don't have to do this," I said. It seemed pretty clear that we were totally gonna do this, whether we needed to or not. Still, I'd hoped to get more of a chance to chat before she sprang at me.

But, nope, I'd barely drawn a breath to talk to her again before she was already flying through the air, knocking me to the dry grass with a surprising amount of force for someone so slight.

I landed funny, my elbow whacking the ground hard and a very unladylike sound exploding from my lips. Irritation flared through me. I'd told myself I'd just neutralize her as fast as I could before questioning her about David, but now I was frustrated and in pain, so I punched out as hard as I could.

Except it wasn't as hard as I could. It was as hard as the me from *before* could, sure, landing on the girl's shoulder with enough impact to make her wince, but she didn't stumble, and she certainly didn't go flying back like she should have after a punch like that.

I blinked, looking at my hand as if it had betrayed me, and then the girl was on me again, hitting with the kind of force I usually wielded. Which *hurt*.

Weakness coursed through me the same way adrenaline and power used to, and I felt the same panicked helplessness I'd felt that night at the pool. Only this time, there was no resurgence of my power, no last-minute reprieve.

Bee was closer now, though, grabbing at the girl with both

hands, and even though she didn't have her Paladin powers, she was still a good head taller than the girl.

Not that it mattered. One well-placed punch, and Bee was falling back to the ground again, crying out, one hand flying to her cheekbone.

Anger flared through me. Rage, really, and I went to get up again. No one hurt Bee on my watch, no matter *how* weak I felt.

Except that rage was no match for Paladin strength. Another kick, some jabs to my back, and I was down *again*, my breath wheezing in and out.

This girl was kicking my butt, and there was nothing I could do other than cover my face with my hands, still trying to punch and kick—I wasn't going out easy—but knowing that it was almost totally ineffectual.

I'm not sure what would have happened if Blythe hadn't come into the tent. Or rather, I'm *too* sure of what would've happened and I didn't want to think about it.

This time, when Blythe did her mind-wipe thing, I just lay there on the grass, trying to breathe, trying not to let my panic show on my face.

Trying not to let Blythe know that as far as powers went, I was now useless.

Blythe managed to get some ice from one of the soda vendors, and when she handed me a freezing bundle wrapped in a paper towel, I pressed it against my lip. "I am so tired of this," I mumbled around the swelling. "Just, like, phenomenally over it at this point."

"Same," Bee said. There was a bruise purpling her cheekbone, and she was holding her own soaking-wet paper towel of ice to her face.

Blythe looked between us for a moment, then rested her eyes on me. "So you had another vision." She nodded at Bee. "But *she* didn't."

Shaking my head, I closed my eyes briefly, my stomach still roiling. "It didn't last long," I replied, and Blythe snorted.

"Doesn't matter how long it lasted. What matters is what you saw."

I sighed and looked up at the hazy blue sky. "It was another cave," I said, my voice flat. "But it was David, not Alaric, in there. He was . . . he was thinking about home."

"A cave?" Blythe asked sharply, her brows drawing together. "So we're too late?"

"Maybe not," I said, even though I definitely wasn't sure of that. "He didn't seem . . . scary, I guess?"

"That has to mean we're getting close again," Bee offered. She was still crouched next to me, one hand on my knee, her skin going pink in the sun. "Going after Dante, we lost him for a bit, but now he's back."

"And still following in Alaric's footsteps," Blythe added. "If he's already found a cave somewhere, started powering up . . ." Trailing off, she twisted the orange plastic bag in her hands. "It would've been better to catch him before all that. Easier."

"I don't think any part of this was ever going to be easy," I muttered, my lip still stinging.

I hadn't liked the way Blythe's face clouded over when she

thought about David already in a cave, doing whatever it was Alaric had done before he wiped out an entire town. I'd always known there was a clock ticking where David was concerned, but now it seemed a lot louder.

"Let's go," I said, rising to my feet, antsy. "We got what we came for, and the sooner we're on the road, the better."

Neither of them argued with me about that, and we made our way back toward the parking lot, the ice melting and dripping onto my chest.

We were almost to the exit but had to wind our way through more tables and tents. There was a whole table of weaponry, and even as I wondered why anyone would want any of this stuff unless they were deeply into *Game of Thrones,* I found myself stopping at the table, staring at the daggers and maces and steel-tipped arrows with something dangerously close to avarice. Becoming a Paladin had certainly given me a better appreciation for these kinds of things, either because I knew just how vital they were to the job, or because I had gotten some kind of passed-down weapons-lust along with all my Paladin powers.

My fingers trailed over the shiny silver hilt of one dagger, and then I moved on to a thin fencing blade, the metal basket decorated with what I guessed were fake jewels, but they were still pretty.

And then I saw the round metal handle sticking out of a box in the back. No, not a handle. A hilt.

Standing there in front of that tent, a bag of ice pressed to my swollen lip, I looked at the top of that sword and felt something thrum deep in my blood. I couldn't even see the whole thing, but I knew that I needed that sword. More than I needed the Coral Shimmer lip gloss I loved, more than I needed the Homecoming Queen crown.

When I lifted a hand to point at it, I realized I was shaking a little, but that might have been from the adrenaline of the fight. Or it could have been something more, something . . . fated.

It wasn't a long blade, nothing all that intimidating, really—other than the fact that it was used for stabbing people, I guess. More like the kind of short sword I'd seen in gladiator movies. And it felt good in my hand.

"How much for the sword?" I asked the guy behind the folding table.

"Um, Harper?" Bee asked. She stood on one side of me, arms held tight to her sides, and I was struck by how not-Bee-like she looked. The frantic pace, the crappy fast-food diet, the stress . . . the three of us now looked less like Cute Girls Headed to the Beach and a lot more like strung-out teenage runaways, albeit ones with decent tans. Anyone observing us would probably think we were only months away from our own Lifetime movie.

"What?" I asked Bee, my eyes still on the sword as the vendor in front of me in a University of Alabama T-shirt glanced over his shoulder.

"Oh," he said, turning more fully toward the box. "Huh, that's . . . You know, I gotta be honest with you, I haven't seen that before."

The alarm bells going off in my head seemed even louder now, and when he walked over and lifted the sword from the box, they were nearly deafening.

It wasn't a fancy sword. There were no jewels on it, and the metal didn't shimmer with unspoken magic or anything like that. It actually looked kind of dull, and while there were some deep grooves on the hilt, it was clearly nothing all that special. Still, everything inside me seemed to reach for it.

The guy hefted the sword, weighing it. "What's a pretty thing like you want with a sword anyway?"

"She's going to use it to castrate guys who ask stupid questions," Blythe answered for me, her voice flat.

"What she said," I told the guy, lifting my chin. His eyes fell to my swollen lip and the ice bag still clutched in my hand, dripping into the dirt.

Clearing his throat, he offered me the sword, handle first. "Fair enough. Since I have no idea where it came from or what it's even made of, I'll give you a discount."

Whether he actually did give me a discount or not, I couldn't say. It's not like I'd ever priced swords or anything, and what he charged was enough to have me grimacing a little bit as I handed over the credit card Mom had given me for emergencies. (Which, okay, I knew she had meant for me to use it for food and shelter and stuff, but I think we can all agree that on *this* trip, a sword was a solid emergency supply.)

But once that sword was in my hand, I knew that I would have paid anything to own it. It felt right clutched against my palm, and I gave a few experimental strokes, earning me some worried looks from all those people who did just want crappy jewelry or a puppy or a cassette tape from 1988.

When we got back to the car, I grabbed an old backpack from

the back of the trunk and a Grove Academy sweatshirt from beside the roadside kit my dad had given me last Christmas. Wrapping the blade gently in the shirt, I placed it in the backpack and
wedged it carefully in the back of the trunk.

But even once the sword was tucked away, I stayed there by
the open trunk, one hand still holding the lid open like I couldn't
quite bring myself to stop looking at it.

"Harper?" Bee asked. Blythe had already gone to sit in the
backseat, so it was just the two of us out there, looking down
into my trunk. "What do you need that sword for?"

I slammed the lid shut. "Just in case."

Chapter 28

We drove for another few hours, heading north. Before Blythe had mind-wiped the girl at the flea market, we'd managed to learn she was from Tennessee, so we headed that way. We found another motel, this one not quite as dire as the one in Mississippi, but still no place I'd choose to stay for very long. Bee had curled up under the blankets after taking a few aspirin, but I was too restless. I felt like we were so close to David, but knowing he was already in a cave made it impossible for me to do anything but think about what we'd do when we found him there.

Blythe was sure it was too late, but I couldn't let myself think that. We'd come all this way, gone through so much, and now that we had Saylor's spell, surely we could fix it?

That thought in mind, I went looking for Blythe. I found her sitting on the edge of the pool, dangling her feet in the bright blue water. For a second, I thought about warning her that there were probably at least a thousand infectious diseases living inside motel pools, but then I decided that, hey, if Blythe wanted to catch syphilis of the foot, that was on her. Me, I was going to sit in one of the lounge chairs.

The plastic creaked when I sat down, and Blythe glanced over her shoulder at me, still moving her feet lazily through the water. "You okay?"

I sighed, unsure how to answer that. Technically, yes, I was fine. The fight today at the flea market had been tough, but the soreness had already faded from my muscles. I still felt like I was about to crawl out of my skin, though. The sense that David was close, but that we were already too late, was making me crazy. I'd wanted to keep driving through the night, but Bee and Blythe were both exhausted, and pointed out that facing David tired was probably not the best idea. Plus Blythe had been quiet all afternoon, and since we needed her at her best for the spell, I wanted to make sure she had enough time to get ready.

Didn't mean I liked it, though.

"I'm not . . . ideal," I finally said, and that made Blythe give a snort of laughter as she pulled her feet up from the pool and turned to face me. Drawing up her knees, she wrapped her arms around her legs. "Your Paladin strength is finally gone. For good, I think," she said, and it wasn't a question.

With a sigh, I leaned back in the chair and looked up at the hazy sky. The air was muggy and thick, buzzing with the sound of insects and the hum of the overhead lights.

"My powers are gone," I agreed. "Like you said they would be. Guess I've finally been away from David too long."

Blythe was looking at me with something close to interest, but less than concern. That was kind of nice. Bee would've bitten her lower lip if I talked about this, a sure sign of worry, but

Blythe? Blythe never seemed all that concerned about what might be bothering me, and that made it easier to actually *say* the things that were bothering me.

"But maybe it's not that," I mused. "Could David be draining me?" I still didn't look at Blythe but focused on a moth currently flinging itself at the nearby sodium lights. "He was able to take Annie's powers away from her."

"Maybe," she replied, a little too quickly for my liking. She could've at least pretended to think about it for a sec.

I sat up and scowled at her.

"He's clearly making new Paladins for some reason," Blythe said. "And if he's making new ones, makes sense that maybe he doesn't want the old one around anymore. Especially when the old one is so determined to keep him from being an Oracle."

"That's not what I'm doing," I fired back. "I don't mind that David can see the future. I *do* mind that seeing the future hurts him. I mind that it could potentially turn him all explode-y and evil, and that if he's anything like Alaric, Pine Grove will be his first target."

Blythe kept watching me, not taking her eyes from my face even when she reached over to slap a mosquito on her arm. "Right," she said. "But he's already all explode-y. And possibly evil, for all you know. And"—she added when I opened my mouth to protest—"you have no way of stopping that. This isn't some kids' movie where the power of love is going to save him from what he really is, Harper. He's a male Oracle. The only other one there's ever been? Explode-y and evil. What makes you think this is something you can control?"

"I can control anything I set my mind to," I replied automatically, and Blythe tipped her head back and laughed, her bright white teeth gleaming. "Oh my God, that sounds like an answer you give to the Model UN or something."

Rolling my eyes, I settled back into my lounge chair. "Fine, make fun," I said. "But it's true. I don't . . . Look, I'm not saying that love *can* save him, or that it will. I'm not saying he isn't already gone. Not in, like, the physical sense." I sighed and looked up at the sky. There were clouds overhead, tinted orange in the streetlights' glow. "The person David was might be gone. I know that. But I have to try."

When I lifted my head, Blythe was watching me, one foot still trailing in the pool. "Can you get that?" I asked her. "That sometimes you have to try even if it seems doomed?"

She looked at me and nodded. "That's what I'm doing," she said at last. "I'm trying something that I'm not sure will work."

"That spell clearly worked," I reminded her. "Dante was powerless *and* couldn't remember his past. So if we can just find David—"

But Blythe shook her head.

"I'm trying to redeem myself," Blythe said, turning back to slip both feet into the water, kicking them back and forth, making little waves. Again, it was so easy for me to imagine the girl she must have been before.

"I did this," she continued, her tone matter-of-fact. "I made him into something unstable and dangerous. Sure, he might've gotten there eventually on his own, but let's not pretend that I didn't speed things up a bit."

She had a point there.

"So, what?" I asked, coming to sit by her and slipping my sandals off. I still wasn't so sure about the less-than-clear aquamarine water of the pool, but I'd take my chances. Sitting next to her, I mimicked her position, hands braced on the concrete, feet dangling in the water. "You think by doing this spell on David and making him not an Oracle anymore, all your sins will be forgiven or something?"

Blythe turned her head and smiled at me, but it was sad. "A spell that has maybe a twenty percent shot of working," she said. "You saw what happened with Dante. You saw how badly that went, and he wasn't some scary, juiced-up super being. Just a boy." She shrugged. "If you still had your powers, maybe I could've pulled it off. Maybe. Or if we'd gotten to him before he went in that cave . . ."

I blinked at her. "The spell," I repeated, almost dumbly. "We found the spell that can drain his powers."

"A spell I might not be able to do," Blythe said, "which means this is going to fall on you in the end." She sounded so calm, so certain, that despite the muggy night I suddenly felt cold.

"What does that mean?"

But I knew the answer before she even spoke.

"You're going to have to kill him."

Chapter 29

"KILL HIM?" I repeated, my voice shooting up about half an octave.

"Mm-hmm." She gave a little nod. "It's our best shot now that he's already in the cave."

For a long moment, I just stared at her, wondering if she was screwing with me. But, no, the moment stretched on without her giving a little wink or breaking at all, until finally I said, "We brought you on this trip to *help* us."

With a roll of those big brown eyes, Blythe turned to look at me again. "Which I *am*, duh. Have you missed the part where David is trying to kill *you*?"

"He isn't," I answered, but that just made her laugh.

"Okay, sure. All those Paladins he's sent after you are the Oracle version of the singing telegram. Got it."

It was beginning to dawn on me that Blythe was most definitely not kidding, and I stood up so fast I nearly slipped on the edge of the pool.

Blythe, however, stayed right where she was, looking up at me like she was legitimately confused. "Harper . . . you knew this was a possibility. At Alexander's, when Bee asked why they didn't just kill Alaric, I saw your face."

She said it so easily that I felt like she had to be right, almost. Like I was the one being irrational here. But I wasn't the one who was calmly talking about murdering someone, and I backed up another step, my heart pounding.

Pulling her feet out of the water, Blythe turned to face me more fully. "Honestly, I thought you got this," she said. "Why else did you buy that sword today?"

The sword. I'd almost forgotten about it, still wrapped in a sweatshirt in the trunk of my car. I couldn't deny the pull I'd felt toward it. Alexander had said that my vision from the fun house—the one where I'd stabbed David—was just what I feared most, not an actual thing that might happen. But facing Blythe now, I felt sick as I wondered if that were the truth.

Blythe must have seen some of that on my face because she leaned in a little, head cocked to the left. "It's the reason I took you to the flea market in the first place."

I shook my head. "No, you said we were looking for some magical rock so you could do the spell Saylor found, and . . ."

The words trailed off as soon as I realized what I was saying. "Magical rock," I scoffed at myself. "Stupid. And it didn't bother you at all that we never found it."

Blythe gave a little shrug. "Because it never existed. I wanted you to find the sword. The one you *needed*. I thought we might need it just in case, but now that you've seen him already in the cave, I understand why you had to have it. Why I *wanted* you to find it."

When I didn't answer, she kept going. "Did you ever think that you were losing your powers not because you were away from him, but because the more dangerous he got, the more you'd be needed to put a stop to him?"

I shook my head, my thoughts whirling, and Blythe crossed her arms over her chest. "Your powers meant you could never hurt the Oracle, only protect him. If you can't protect him anymore, it's because he's become such a danger that he has to be dealt with, Harper. I wasn't sure of it until today, but seeing him in the cave? Your powers going out for good? Those things are connected."

"You don't know that—" I started, even though everything she was saying made a terrible kind of sense.

And she knew it, too, because she lifted her hand to cut me off. "You and I, we do what needs to be done, Harper. It's who we are. Did you know that back before all this happened to me, I was SGA president at my school, too? We didn't have cheerleaders, but I was first-chair flute in the school symphony, and I was on just about every committee there was. Prom, Students Against Drunk Driving, the Big Sisters program . . ." She ticked them off on her fingers. "And commitment like that is what makes both of us so good at this stuff. It's why we were chosen."

I shook my head, not wanting to have anything in common with her right now. "No," I said. "Those powers . . . they were forced on me, and I'm guessing they were forced on you, too."

She just shrugged in that way she did, tilting her head to the other side. "Forced, fated . . . all works out the same. Point is, we're the type of girls who do what they have to do, and stopping David is what I have to do. You know what Alaric turned into. And now we know that not only is David following in his exact footsteps, they're also the only two Oracles ever *born* to Oracles. That means David is more powerful than any of us thought. More dangerous."

Once again, her voice was so even and calm, her face almost eerily placid, that I felt like I was the one who was nuts. Still, I heard myself say, "This isn't what you have to do."

"Of course it is. I told you," she said slowly and patiently, the way you talk to really little kids or people who speak a different language. "I'm. Redeeming. Myself."

My shoes dangled from my fingertips, and one dropped to the concrete with a muted *thwack*. "But this isn't redeeming yourself," I argued. "Redeeming means . . . it means *fixing* what you did wrong, not stabbing what you did wrong in the face. Okay, wait, that didn't come out right, but you know what I mean."

I pointed one sandal at her, and Blythe finally got to her feet, swatting my shoe out of her face. "Harper, this is how we fix this, don't you get that? What do you think all this journeying around has been about?"

I shook my head, not getting it. "Finding David. To make him stop, not to murder him."

Blythe took a step forward, and when I moved backward, she lifted her hands in entreaty. "I didn't want it to come to this either, Harper. When I found that spell, I thought we had the answer. Killing him was always . . ." Trailing off, she looked up at the low clouds, tinted orange by the lights around the motel. "A last resort, I guess. It's just that it's too late now."

"I don't believe anything you say," I muttered, and took another step back.

But Blythe kept coming, her dark eyes bright in the glow from the sodium lights above the pool. "I was looking for another way. But there isn't one."

"What about the other spell?" I asked, and she blinked. "The one that Dante mentioned," I said. "Whatever it was that was darker and scarier than the power-wipe spell. What about that one?"

Blythe sniffed, shaking her head. "It won't help," she said, her voice tight.

"You're always going on about what a badass Mage you are," I said, shaking my head, "and now you're telling me you can't do one simple spell?"

"It's not simple!" Blythe shouted, her hands clenched into fists, her voice tight. "Alexander managed it on Dante, but Dante had hardly any powers. Just some Mage skills he picked up from *the internet*. Trying to do this to a full-blown Oracle who's gone rogue?"

This time when she looked at me, I could see tears in her eyes. "I. Can't," she said again. "It's too dangerous. For you, for me, for Bee. What if it just amps him up more? I gave Dante powers he never even really *had*, and we saw how that went."

"Ryan," I said, grasping for anything. "If you can't do it, we'll let him try." But Blythe just shook her head.

"We don't have time. Now that your powers are gone, now that he's in the cave, the only way is to kill him. Put this behind us once and for all."

For the first time, something sparked in her eyes. In anyone else, I would have said it was anger, but in Blythe, it was that tiniest hint of crazy that I knew all too well could blossom into full-blown whackjobbery. "Your last duty as his Paladin is setting him free."

And then she frowned a little. "Although, I guess . . . without powers, you're not actually his Paladin anymore."

The words stung.

But my voice was as steady as hers when I replied, "I don't think it's the powers that make the Paladin, to be honest. I think it's the determination."

Blythe smiled briefly at that, which just intensified the whole crazy-eyes thing she had going on. "And how determined are you, Harper Price?"

By now, she was very close to me, hands on her hips. Through the triangles made by her elbows, I could see the bright turquoise water of the pool behind her, and I didn't let myself think. I might not have superstrength or superspeed anymore, but I still knew how to Mean Girl when the situation called for it.

"Hella," I answered, and with that, I charged forward, shoving with all my might.

I'm not a big girl, but Blythe was even smaller and more delicate, plus, as she'd said herself, her school didn't have cheerleading. Plus I'd caught her by surprise.

She shrieked as she fell backward into the water, her hands

grabbing at me, but I was too quick, moving out of her embrace before she could tug me in, too. She was light enough (and I'd pushed hard enough) that she went out near the middle of the pool.

I didn't see her hit the water, only heard the splash as I bolted from the pool, running down the cement sidewalk in my bare feet, sandals abandoned on the pool deck. Luckily I still had tennis shoes in the room.

Even more luckily, I had barely unpacked today, so when Bee let me in after I pounded on the door, it was an easy thing to just grab my bag.

Bee, unfortunately, was not as organized.

"Um, what are we doing?" she asked, her phone still held near her jaw as I started throwing her things in her Vera Bradley tote. "Where's Blythe?"

I shook my head. "We have to go," I said. "Now."

Look, Bee is not a perfect best friend. She once dated a guy I could barely stand, she listened to truly obnoxious music, and I had caught her making out with my ex in a supply closet. Plus she'd lied to me and helped David escape town, which had led to this whole mess.

But when it counted, Bee always came through.

"Call you back," she said to who I assumed was Ryan, and then gathered up the rest of her things, moving as fast as I was without asking a single question. It took her about thirty seconds to throw all she'd gotten out into her tote, but that was about ten seconds too long. We'd just slung our bags over our shoulders when Blythe appeared in the doorway, soaking wet and, surprisingly, nowhere near as angry as I thought she would be.

"Harper," she started, but I could see her fingers flexing at her side, and while there was no anger pouring off her, there was something else, something a lot scarier than anger.

Magic.

Chapter 30

WE WERE all frozen there, me and Bee in the room, our bags still on our shoulders, Blythe standing in the doorway, her fingers still flexing, water dripping from her hair. We'd spent enough time together over the past few days that she'd started to feel like my friend, and only now did I realize how stupid that had been. Blythe wasn't Ryan. She sure as heck wasn't Bee. She was a girl who did things for her own reasons, reasons I couldn't possibly understand, and for all that she might say we were alike, I knew now that we couldn't be. I could never be this ruthless, this . . . what had she said?

Determined.

"We're leaving," I told Blythe now. "Without you. And to be honest, I don't care where you go from here, but you're not coming with us."

Blythe gave me that little half smile that had become so familiar. "Do you really think I don't know where you're going? God's sake, Harper, I feel David, too. Maybe not as clearly, but still. The tightness in the chest, the headaches . . ."

She did and she had magic to boot, but—I remembered as my hip started to tingle—so did we.

I had no idea how Ryan's mark might work, but it was supposed to act against Blythe's magic if we were in danger, and I felt pretty sure that we were in danger now, no matter how much Blythe might smile and say we weren't.

The wind was picking up outside, and I could hear the first few patters of raindrops on the sidewalk and roof, but the electric feeling in the air had nothing to do with the storm, and everything to do with the girl standing in front of us, keeping us from leaving.

Ryan and I had talked about how the wards would work—the one Bee and I both had, and the one I wasn't telling anyone about. I didn't have to mutter a spell or anything, just . . . think about what I wanted to happen.

Blythe was still talking, her hands held out in that conciliatory way people use when they're trying to come across like rational people, but seeing as how the first words out of Blythe's mouth had been "Killing David is the only solution here," I wasn't sure that "rational" was even in her vocabulary.

"What?" Bee squawked next to me. "We're here to rescue him."

Blythe rolled her eyes, stepping farther into the room. "And you can't. The spell is too big a risk. Didn't everything with Dante prove that? This is unstable magic we're working with, and an unstable Oracle on top of everything else. Like I said, if we'd gotten to him before the cave . . ."

It was probably just a trick of the light, but I could swear I saw her lower lip wobble a bit before she said, "I honestly did try to help you. All of you. But there *isn't a way.* There just isn't. Except this."

I shook my head, my fingers falling to the tattoo on my back. "There's always another way," I said, and Blythe's gaze followed the movement of my hand.

Her own hand shot up, and I felt a pulse of magic, but it was like Bee and I were behind protective glass. The power bumped harmlessly off us, and Blythe looked at her hand much the same way I'd looked at mine earlier today—confused, kind of betrayed.

"What did you do?" she asked, almost wondering, but before I could reply, she tried again. This time, whatever spell she was pulling up was stronger, and I felt it like a fist pushing at my sternum, but still, Ryan's ward held.

Blythe dropped both of her hands, sucking in a deep breath through her nose. "Harper," she said, clearly losing her patience, "I don't want to hurt you. The whole point of this is to keep the Oracle from *killing* you. Don't do—"

Her words were abruptly cut off as Bee, who had edged around behind Blythe while Blythe's focus was on me, brought a lamp down on her head.

It was maybe not the most elegant of moves, but it worked, and Blythe's eyes rolled back as she slid to the floor.

We didn't hesitate this time, grabbing our bags and hurrying out of the room.

It was raining heavily now, one of those "gully washers" as my aunts would say, the kind that start and stop all of a sudden in southern summers. My car was parked in the farthest corner of the lot, so Bee and I were just as soaked as Blythe had been by the time we got to it.

Reaching into the backseat, I pulled Blythe's bag out, tossing it to the sidewalk. I might have pushed her in a pool and Bee might have hit her with a lamp, but we weren't *terrible* people. Granted, all her stuff was going to get wet, but I figured Blythe could sort that out.

That done, we got in the car, and I drove out of the parking lot like I was fleeing the scene of a crime.

Which I guessed I was, technically. Bee's lamp had definitely hit her hard enough to qualify as assault and battery. I did tell myself not to feel guilty about what had just happened, though. I was protecting David, and that was my job whether I had powers or not. But I thought Blythe had been telling the truth when she said she'd looked for other ways to save him. She was scared, or maybe she just didn't want it badly enough.

I was scared, too, believe me, but I was also willing to do anything, no matter how risky it might be.

"So do you have a plan?" Bee asked, and I appreciated that she waited until we'd gotten to the interstate before asking me that. It showed a certain amount of faith I really needed right now. Rain was beating on the windows, and I had the wipers turned on as high as they would go, adding this frantic feeling to everything. My heart was pounding, my hands were shaking, and all I could think was how close we'd come to screwing up. If I had led Blythe to David and she'd killed him . . . I could hardly even think about it.

"If I can get to him," I told her, "if I can just *talk* to him, maybe . . . maybe we won't even need the spell. Any spell. Maybe there's enough David in there to overrule the Oracle."

Bee was quiet for a long time before she finally said, "Harper, you know that's crazy."

I did. It was completely irrational and stupid and nothing like me. I was the girl who made a spreadsheet for her first-week-of-school wardrobe, for goodness' sake. The girl who had a plan for everything.

But from the very beginning, nothing about any of this had gone to plan. Maybe it was time to throw out the rule book and trust my instincts.

Instincts that could, I was willing to admit, get me totally killed.

"I have to try," I told Bee. "Even if it doesn't work. Even if I . . ."

I didn't want to say it out loud, but I thought again of the sword in the trunk.

Reaching over, Bee squeezed my hand where it clutched the steering wheel. "Okay," she said. "So since plans and calendars and schedules haven't worked, we'll try being nuts for a change."

She smiled at me, and I wanted to smile back, but I was way too worried for that now. Besides, I needed to think about where we were headed.

I focused on that vision I'd had, remembering what I could from those moments when David's mind and mine were linked.

"North," I said to Bee now, my fingers flexing on the steering wheel, the answer floating up through my brain. "He's north, in Tennessee."

Bee glanced over at me, the rain making strange patterns on her face. "Blythe can sense him, too," she said. "She said so."

I nodded and thought again of the sword in the trunk.

"We just need to get there first," I said. "And now we have a head start and also, you know, a car, which is something Blythe is definitely lacking at the moment."

Bee made a little noise in the back of her throat, turning to look at the rain-slicked road ahead of us. "I still wouldn't count her out."

Determined, I thought again, remembering the look in Blythe's eyes.

"Me, neither," I told Bee. "But we just have to get there first."

Chapter 31

"Do y'all need a map?"

The park ranger in front of me was maybe the perkiest person I had ever seen in my life, and seeing as how I had been a cheerleader *and* in a pageant, that was saying a lot.

"Yes, please," I said, trying to smile and not shatter into about a billion pieces. Because David was here. I could feel it, and I thought Bee could, too. It was like a constant weight in my chest, a second heartbeat thudding away in there. My Paladin strength and quickness might be gone, but it was clear some thread still connected me to David.

I had to admit he'd chosen a good place, too. The visitor center was a tall, octagonal room with the information desks against one wall, but windows surrounded the rest of the space. They looked out on a wall of green, branches pressing so close to the glass it felt like we were in a tree house. And beyond the trees were the mountains, even though we couldn't really see them from here. The peaks weren't especially high, and the heavy forest blocked most of the view. Still, the mountains were there, and in those mountains, there were caves, like the ones the ancient Oracles had lived in in Greece.

Who knew that David Stark of all people could be such a drama queen?

Bee had wandered to the big display in the middle of the room, a low table containing a topographical map of the region, and once I had my own paper map, I joined her. I ran my fingers over the ridges and valleys of the mountain—okay, really, the super big hill—we were about to climb, and wished I'd eaten more this morning. I hadn't eaten when Bee, Blythe, and I had stopped yesterday at the motel, either, and my stomach had been too jumpy to even think about anything more than a bag of trail mix from a gas station. But now, looking at this hill, I felt like something more substantial had been called for.

Especially if it was going to be my last meal.

Turning away from the model, I took in a deep breath through my nose. I couldn't think like that, not right now. I was so totally not going to die. *David* was so totally not going to die. I was going to save David or at least talk him out of going all mega Oracle and destroying Pine Grove . . . somehow, and then we were all going to go home and put this behind us.

I just hadn't figured out the *how* yet.

Bee and I left the visitor center, stepping out into the thick heat of late-July Tennessee. Despite the fact that we were technically in the mountains and there was a cover of green over everything, the leaves blocking out almost all of the direct sunlight, this was still summer in the South, which meant I was sweating every place a girl can sweat.

Next to me, Bee shifted her backpack and slid her sunglasses down from the top of her head. "So . . . we're doing this?" she asked, and I looked up at the trail stretching in front of us. It started just beyond the parking lot, a cheerful brown wooden sign reminding us that we were taking our lives into our own hands, and I nearly laughed at that. Of course, whoever had put up the sign was worried about people falling or possibly getting mauled by black bears, not facing down a supernatural boy in a cave.

I swallowed hard, my mouth dry. "We are," I said to Bee.

We'd joked about this whole thing being a quest right from the very beginning, like we were knights-errant on an impressive journey, not a group of girls driving through the back roads of the South, eating gas station food and staying in creepy motels. But as Bee and I started climbing up the trail leading into the woods, for the first time, it genuinely *felt* like a quest. The forest was quiet, and there were no other people on the path, probably because it was hotter than Satan's armpit. Or maybe they'd felt something. Not as strongly as I felt it, of course, but something nonetheless, a sense of "wrongness," like Saylor's brother had described.

I could feel something, too. The higher we climbed, the deeper we got into the woods, the stronger the feeling got. I wasn't sure how long we hiked, ignoring hunger pangs in my stomach and the scratches of thorns and brambles. I was glad I'd decided to wear jeans even though they were heavy and damp with sweat. But that discomfort was nothing compared to every other sensation. I knew David was close. I couldn't explain *how* I knew, exactly. Just that the feeling, almost as though I had two heartbeats, seemed stronger, heavier.

Now instead of making our way through undergrowth, we were on hard-packed dirt, but the way we needed to go was steep, and I felt my thighs and calves protest as I headed up the ridge.

Behind me, Bee gave a little gasp, and I turned to see her stumble, one hand flailing out as pebbles slid from beneath her feet. Without thinking, I reached down to grab her outstretched arm. Bee was about half a foot taller than me, and heavier, plus she had gravity on her side. Our hands locked together, and I gritted my teeth as I caught her and kept her upright.

But the force of my pull sent me stumbling backward so that I fell hard on my butt, wincing as a loose twig scraped the exposed skin of my ankle.

For a moment, we just sat there, breathing hard, in the middle of the trail, me sitting, Bee half sprawled on the ground. My shoulder ached, and my leg stung, and I had knocked the breath out of myself with that hard fall, so I was nearly wheezing.

If ever there was an appropriate moment for swearwords, this was it. We were halfway up a mountain in Tennessee, going after my magical ex-boyfriend, a guy who had sent superpowered assassins after me. We had ditched the one person who could've maybe helped us in all of this because I hadn't wanted her to hurt David, but what if he was going to hurt *me*?

Lowering my head to my hands, I took a deep breath through my nose. "Bee," I said, my voice wavering, and to my horror, I could feel stinging at the backs of my eyes, a thickness in my throat. "I effed this up."

I did not say "effed." I said the actual word. And it felt so good that I thought maybe I needed to say it again. Lots.

Lifting my head, I looked at Bee and tears spilled down my cheeks. "My effing powers are effing *gone,* and now I've got us into this effed-up situation, and I have *no effing clue* what the eff I'm going to do once we find David. Not a single. Effing. Idea."

Bee's eyes had gone wide, but I wasn't sure if it was from my confession or the fact that I had just used that word so many times. And honestly, whichever it was, I did not give an eff.

I was openly crying now, and I shook my head. "I don't think I can do this," I said, and I wasn't sure if I meant I couldn't save David or that I couldn't bring myself to hurt him if it came to that. Honestly, it could have been both. Earlier today, when we'd left the car, I'd almost left the sword behind. Sure, if there ended up being other Paladins in the cave, I might need it, but there was always the thought at the back of my mind that I might have to use it on David.

Rising to her feet, Bee crossed over to me and took me firmly by the shoulders. "You can," she said, squeezing for emphasis. "Harper, listen to me. Your powers are great and all, and I'm not going to pretend I don't really wish they were working about right now, but . . . being a Paladin isn't what's going to save David. *You* can save him because he loves you. Because you love him."

Sniffling, I rolled my eyes. "That's very Disney-movie of you, Bee."

I'd meant to make her smile, but she just gave me another little shake. "I'm serious. Even if your powers had been gone before we started on this whole thing, I would've gone with you."

She said the words so quietly, so simply, that something in my chest seemed to give way. My becoming a Paladin had hurt Bee. It had gotten her kidnapped and superpowered and nearly killed. But she was still looking at me like she believed in me, and that gave me the strength to nod, reaching out to rest my hands on her forearms.

"Okay," I said. "You're right. I can do this."

I repeated the words, almost like a mantra. Satisfied, Bee gave a little smile and stepped back, hoisting her pack.

"So how much farther, do you think?" she asked.

I turned to jerk my chin at the trail winding its way up to a wall of stone and green above us. "Not much farther at all," I told her, and took a deep breath. "We're here."

Chapter 32

HERE IS A THING you should know about me: I really hate caves. Maybe it's the damp and the dark, maybe it's the thought of being underground. Who can say? The point is, I've always avoided them, not even going on my class field trip to DeSoto Caverns in the third grade. I'd missed underground mini-golf and a laser show because I hated caves so much.

Which meant that walking into the mouth of that huge fissure in the rock was one of the hardest things I've ever had to do. Bee and I made our way up the hill, and even though the air was loud with the sound of buzzing insects, the breeze through the leaves, and our own breathing, it seemed weirdly quiet and still.

The cave was nearly hidden behind a wall of branches and vines, but I pushed those aside, staring into the darkness in front of me. Bee stepped forward, too, shifting her backpack on her shoulder, but I stopped and turned toward her, taking a deep breath.

"I know you're not going to like this," I started, and she immediately shook her head, almost glaring at me.

"Harper, no," she said firmly, but I reached out and wrapped my fingers around her biceps, making her look down into my face.

"This is something I have to do alone," I told her. "You've come all this way with me, and I couldn't have done any of it without you, you know that, but this—" Breaking off, I turned to look over my shoulder at the gaping mouth of limestone behind me. "This is on me."

Bee blinked a few times, and her eyes were bright, her face pale. "You don't have your powers anymore," she said, and her voice trembled.

"Neither do you," I reminded her, giving her arms a squeeze. "And I can't risk you getting hurt. Not again."

I wasn't sure I'd ever stop feeling guilty for what had happened to Bee the night of Cotillion, and while I knew I could never make it up to her, this at least let me feel like I was trying. I remembered the way Blythe's eyes had shone as she'd talked about "redeeming" herself, and while she and I might have really different ideas about what redemption meant, I understood why it was so important to her.

"I've screwed up a lot of things," I told Bee now. "I've lied and I've hurt people I've cared about, and I've made some less-than-stellar decisions about, like, everything, basically. But this?" I nodded back toward the cave. "This I can do. This I *have* to do. And I need you to wait out here."

Despite that rousing speech, I could tell Bee still wanted to argue. But then, I would've argued, too. That's what best friends do.

But then she looked past me up at the wall of stone, and took a deep breath. "I hate this," she said. "Like, more than I hate snakes or humidity or AP Calculus." And then she looked back down, our eyes meeting. "But if this is what you have to do, it's what you have to do."

My throat felt tight as I reached down and took her hands, squeezing them. "Best squire ever," I said, and she tried to laugh, but the sound was kind of choked, and then she was hugging me hard.

"Ten minutes," she said.

"Fifteen," I countered, and she rolled her eyes.

"Fine, fifteen, but any longer than that, and I'm coming after you."

Nodding, I turned back to the mouth of the cave. The air wafting out was cool, and goose bumps rose up on my arms. I reached over my shoulder, my fingers finding the hilt of the sword, still wrapped in its towel, and I took some comfort from the weight of it.

I gave one last look to Bee, who gave me a tight smile, and then, taking another deep breath, I stepped forward.

The rock was slick underneath my feet. Tennis shoes were not exactly the best footwear for this kind of thing, I thought, and I felt a hysterical laugh bubble up in my throat. Man, it seemed like a lot of this Paladin business came down to the right shoes.

Almost a year ago, I'd lain on the floor of the school bathroom, my pink heel clutched in my hands, waiting for someone to kill me. He hadn't. I had killed him. I had won.

If I killed David today, it wouldn't feel the slightest bit like winning.

The cave I found myself standing in wasn't nearly as big as I'd thought it would be, and I took a moment getting my bearings and really wishing I'd gotten a rabies vaccine before I'd left for this trip. While the ceiling of the cave was lost to the darkness, I couldn't help but envision roughly a million bats overhead, and it made me shudder.

But then I realized that, while I could feel David nearby, I sure couldn't *see* him, and the cave seriously didn't seem to be all that huge, so where—

And then I saw it: another little opening in the back of the cave, so small that I thought I might have to hold my breath to squeeze through.

David, I reminded myself again, which, seriously, was starting to feel like another kind of mantra. Like, if I could just keep repeating his name, picturing his face, I could get through this thing.

I took my pack off, knowing it would make it harder to squeeze through, wondering how David had managed to get himself in there. He wasn't a big guy, but he still had to be wider through the shoulders than I was, and I eyed the crack in the rock speculatively.

My pack made a loud *clank* as it hit the rock floor, and I pulled the sword out of it, moving forward.

Luckily, the passage wasn't as narrow as I'd thought, and once I got inside, I moved through fairly easily, the sword clutched in my hands, pressed tight against my body. For a second, I had a vision of those old tombs of knights you sometimes see, their swords laid out along their torsos, and I wasn't sure if I wanted to laugh or cry.

If being a Paladin had taught me anything, it was that you could never really prepare for everything. I could think about it, of course, and I had, a lot, over the course of this trip. There had been nights lying in motel beds, staring at popcorn ceilings, and wondering what I would do when I finally saw David again.

Blythe hadn't lied when she'd said that I'd known it might come to killing him. Of course I had, no matter how many times I tried not to think of it. For the past six months, I'd gotten so good at telling myself that I could handle everything, that the worst would never happen.

It seemed like I'd been wrong every time.

As I made my way through that narrow tunnel, taking deep breaths, my palms sweaty around the sword, I reminded myself that I had no idea what I was about to come face-to-face with. That for all I knew, I was minutes away from having to drive a sword through the heart of the boy I loved.

So, yeah, I was prepared for a lot of things when the passage-way finally opened up into a wider space.

Prepared for anything but what I saw: David, standing there in plaid pants and a black sweater. Light was pouring in from a hole high in the ceiling, and it made his sandy hair look gold.

But that was the only gold thing about him. There was no light in his eyes, nothing but the normal blue irises behind his glasses, and when he smiled at me, the sword slipped from my suddenly numb fingers.

"Hi, Pres."

Chapter 33

I SWEAR I could still hear a faint echo from where the sword had clattered to the ground, but over that, there was the sound of my own blood rushing in my ears and a slight, broken sob coming from my lips.

He was here. He was here and he was *fine.* Just the David I had known, and my own relief carried me forward until I was right in front of him, my arms around his neck before I could let myself think.

"You're okay," I said, breathing him in. He smelled familiar, like soap and the ink from the printers in the newspaper room.

It was weird, I thought, burying my face in his neck, that after all that time, that smell should still cling to him, that he would be wearing clothes much more suited for the winter than a southern summer, and even as I hugged him tight to me, I knew.

I knew.

"Easy there." He laughed against my temple even as he hugged me back. "You're going to wrinkle my sweet sweater."

I laughed, the sound watery because tears were already choking me. "Couldn't make it any worse."

He pulled back then, his hand coming up to cup my face. "I missed you," he told me, and I felt like I couldn't breathe. This wasn't real—I wasn't sure how he was doing it, or if it was even him doing this particular trick—but just for a moment, I didn't care.

"I missed you, too," I told him, and then I was on my tiptoes, pressing my mouth to his.

His kiss was as familiar as that soap smell that clung to him, and I tightened my hands on his shoulders, thinking back to that first night he'd kissed me at Cotillion.

He had kissed me then because we'd thought one or both of us might die that night, and this kiss had some of that same desperation. If this was just an illusion, it was a good one, and I'd take it.

When we parted, David looked down at me, smiling fondly, his thumb running across my lower lip. "This seems like a time for egregious felicitations," he said, and I sucked in a breath. It was an old joke between us, using the words we'd each missed in spelling bees growing up, and one that made me think, just for a minute, that maybe I was wrong about him not really being him. He looked like David and smelled like David, and now he was making jokes like David. In that moment, I suddenly wanted him to *be* David so badly that it hurt.

That was the worst part. Admitting that after all of this, after trying to find him and stop whatever Oracle-induced craziness he had going on, what I'd really wanted was to see *him* again. It felt like such a hard thing to admit for some reason, that it had been the girl in me driving this whole thing on, not the Paladin.

Raising my head to look at David, I studied his face. It was a face I'd seen every day of my life, seemed like, and one I couldn't bear to think of not seeing again.

"I wish we hadn't wasted all that time hating each other," I told him, and he laughed again. It was his laugh, his eyes, his freckles scattered across his nose, even if it wasn't really him.

"I never hated you," he said softly, and I smiled even as my heart broke. If this wasn't the real David, was there some part of him still in this? Was he somehow projecting the him he'd been? I kind of hoped so.

"Oh, I totally hated you," I told him. "Didn't fake that a bit."

He made a sort of huffing, disdainful sound that I had heard a thousand times, and I wondered if I'd ever hear it again after today.

Then David tilted his chin down, and for a second, I thought he was going to kiss me again. I definitely wanted him to.

But instead, he looked into my eyes and murmured, "Leave me here, Harper."

"Is this even the real you?" I asked, and he sighed again, the corners of his mouth quirking down quickly. Another familiar expression that made my chest hurt.

"Does it matter?" he asked, and I stepped back, my head starting to clear. It had been nice to believe in this for a little while, but I couldn't keep pretending, no matter how much I wanted to. This was just another distraction, and while I didn't know how he was doing it, I knew I couldn't give in anymore.

"Yes," I said, and now there was a good two feet of space between us. "Because I can't just walk out of here and pretend I said good-bye to the real you, when actual you is still in here."

A crease appeared between David's brows. "Harper, isn't it better to remember me this way?" he asked, and look, I wanted to say yes. I wanted to kiss him one more time and not have to confront whatever scary things might be waiting for me in this cave.

But that wasn't who I was, not as a Paladin, not as a person.

"I can't," I told him now, and his frown deepened. It seemed like he was shimmering for a second, and I suddenly realized I could see the rock wall of the cave behind him. *Through* him.

"This is all that's left of me, Harper," he said, but his voice was faint. "What's waiting for you farther on . . . that's not me anymore."

My eyes stung with unshed tears. I believed him, that this . . . vision or whatever it was of him was the last, dying remnants of the real David, saying good-bye. Maybe because he loved me, maybe because he didn't want me stopping the Oracle.

Knowing David, it was probably a little bit of both.

"I can't," I said again. And then, firmer, "I *won't*."

With that, I bent to pick up my fallen sword, and then I stepped forward, moving through him as he faded from sight completely.

Head held high, I walked out of the open cave space and toward a narrow fissure in the back wall of the cave. The farther I went, the brighter the passageway got, and for a moment, I wondered if there was a hole in the ceiling, opening up to the sky, like it had in the other chamber. But then I realized that, no, the light wasn't coming from above, but from out in front of me. And it wasn't the soft yellow glow of the sun, but the bright, unnatural gold I'd seen spilling out of David's eyes over and over again. I remembered the way he'd looked in the grips of a vision and tried to tell myself I was prepared for whatever it was I was going to see when I reached the end of this path.

I was wrong.

The narrow passage gave way to another, larger open chamber, so high the ceiling was lost in the gloom despite the light.

David—the real David—sat in the middle of this chamber. His clothes were ragged and dirty, with holes in his T-shirt and in the knees of his jeans. I had a feeling they were the same clothes he'd been wearing the night he left Pine Grove, and for some reason, that made me the saddest of all. What had he been through since that last night? What had happened to him?

"David," I called, the name echoing around the cave, seeming to lodge in my heart as I said it.

Because it wasn't David sitting in front of me. Despite the ragged clothes, the hair that still stuck up in weird tufts, the truly terrible footwear, the person in front of me wasn't the boy I had loved. He was . . . a thing.

An Oracle.

And then his bright eyes turned to me, mouth opening.

For one heartbeat, stupid as it sounds, I thought maybe I was wrong. Maybe he wasn't as far gone as I'd thought, and he was going call me "Pres," and things would be okay. That the illusion he'd created was close to the real thing.

Instead, he looked at me with those blinding eyes and intoned, *"Paladin."*

Chapter 34

I swallowed hard, my mouth dry.

"You used to have a different name for me," I said, my voice sounding thin and tight. "Do you remember that? You called me Pres."

David—or the thing that had been David—didn't move, didn't even give any sense that he'd heard me.

Cold sweat was dripping down my back, but I made myself step a little closer. "Of course, I'm sure there were other things you called me that weren't nearly as nice, but you usually didn't say those to my face."

"Where is the Mage?" David asked, the words echoing, and I bit back a sigh.

"Which one? Ryan or Blythe? We have two, you know, and it's a total—"

David flung out one hand, a bolt of golden light shooting from his palm and cracking against the rock behind me. Tiny pebbles and dust flew, and I flinched away.

"That's a new trick," I said, wishing I didn't sound so shaky. "Where did you pick that up?"

"You know the Mage I'm speaking of," David said, and I wondered if we'd spend these last moments like this, talking in circles around each other.

But then maybe these weren't the last moments. Maybe there was a chance that I could actually find the David still inside him.

And if there wasn't . . .

I shifted my grip on the sword. The metal was cold despite my sweaty palms, the little grooves on the hilt biting into my skin. That was good, though. The discomfort made me feel grounded and aware, the same way I'd always liked my ponytail just a little too tight at cheerleading practice. Minor pain kept you from focusing on major pain. In cheerleading, that had been the stretch and burn of muscles.

Now the pain was all in my heart.

"Blythe isn't here," I said to him. "We left her behind when we realized what she wanted to do to you. David, we're here to help you."

He tilted his head just a little to the left, like he was trying to hear something from a distance. "We?" he repeated.

"Bee and I. And Ryan, too, he . . . he helped us before we left. David, there are people who care about you, people who want to save you."

A little smile twisted his mouth, but there was nothing David-like in it. "Save me? From what?"

I faltered, my sneakers skidding a little on the damp rock. "From . . . this. From hurting people, from not being who you really are. David, there aren't any more Ephors. There's no one to use you or who wants to control you, and if we could find some way to help you get rid of your powers—"

Another bolt of light, another *crack*, and a showering of little rocks.

"This is who I am," he intoned, the voice his and not his all at the same time. "This is *what* I am."

I shook my head. "No. You're a lot more than this, David, and you deserve an actual life."

There was a low humming noise, and I wondered if it had been there the whole time. I could feel the hairs on my arms standing up, a chill slithering down my spine, and my hands tightened on the hilt of the sword.

"You saw this," I said, my voice thick with tears. "I don't know if you even remember it anymore, but that first day we met Blythe, you sat in my car and told me you used to have bad dreams about me."

David didn't move, didn't give any sign of even hearing me. His eyes were nothing but glowing circles, and his whole body was lined in light. Still, I made myself keep going.

"You said we were fighting, but we weren't angry. We were sad."

Dropping one hand from the sword, I dashed at the tears on my face. "And you were right. I'm not angry. Not about any of it."

"Then why are you holding a sword?"

David's voice was still doing that echo thing, like there was more than one voice coming out of his mouth. I'd heard that before, of course. Whenever he had a vision, he tended to sound like that. But now, I wasn't sure if it was the acoustics in the cave, or the power he'd developed, but it was like a chorus of voices now.

Still, that question . . . it hadn't sounded like the Oracle. For all those voices making all that noise, there was a little edge, just the tiniest hint of snark, which sounded like David.

I tried not to let that make me too hopeful. So he sounded like himself. So there was still a part of him in there. I'd known that, right? It's why he'd come here to hide himself, trying to stop this from happening. But I hadn't been able to let that happen. I'd had to find him and see for myself, and now I was going to pay the price for that.

Both my hands were wrapped tight around the hilt of the sword again, but I made myself sound as light as I could as I called back, "Oh, you know me. Always have to make sure I have the right accessory. A sword just felt appropriate for visiting my magical ex-boyfriend in a cave. Although now I'm wondering if it isn't a bit much."

There was no hint of anything in David's eyes—he didn't really have eyes now—but I thought there was the slightest hint of a smile.

It wasn't much, but it was something.

"Did you ever read *A Wrinkle in Time?*" I called out to him now. "You probably did because like every smart kid loves that book, and you were the smartest kid I knew. Do you remember at the end, when Meg saves her little brother by reminding him who he is? Telling him she loves him?"

Still no reaction, but I moved closer, letting the sword drop to my side.

"I don't know if I believe that can actually work. I'd like to, obviously. And I do love you."

The glow in David's eyes didn't really dim, it couldn't have, but I could have sworn something flickered across his face.

I kept going. "And Saylor loved you. Not the Oracle you, although it probably started there. But she loved you the *person*. Even Alexander—" I broke off, wondering if I should mention what we'd discovered, that Alexander was David's father, but I wasn't sure it would do any good right now. Instead, I just said, "He tried to save you from this, too. Me, Bee, Ryan . . . we all looked for a way to save *you*, not because you were an Oracle, but because you're *you*."

By now, I had come close enough that I could almost reach out and touch him, and to my surprise, David rose to his feet, facing me almost uncertainly.

"Just try," I said, my voice cracking. "Try to remember who you were before all of this. We've looked through spell books, and we've tried rituals, and none of it has worked. But maybe that's because we can't fix this after all. Maybe only you can do that."

He still didn't move, but I was sure the light in his eyes was dimmer now, and hope surged in my chest, so sharp it ached.

"David," I said, reaching out with one hand. It was trembling, but I kept it out there anyway, waiting. Hoping.

Slowly, he raised his own hand. Like the rest of him, it glowed faintly, fingers outlined in light, but when his fingers touched mine, they were warm and solid and . . . normal.

My throat ached, and I moved closer. He was in there, I knew he was. We could *fix* this, somehow, if we just—

"Harper!"

I turned, startled, to see Blythe behind me, her yellow dress bright in the gloom, Bee right on her heels.

"Blythe?" I asked, confused. How had she gotten here, and why?

David's hand fell away from mine, and his features twisted into a snarl, eyes glowing so brightly I winced and threw one hand up against the glare.

I could feel magic building, and David lifted his hand again, the one that had just been touching mine. Light lined his fingers as they moved, pointing toward Blythe.

And Bee.

I didn't think.

I raised the sword and lunged forward.

Chapter 35

Saylor had trained me in sword fighting, but that had been back when I actually had my powers, and then, I'd been swinging a sword at practice dummies, not someone I loved.

Not David.

But I swung now for all I was worth, even as every muscle in my arms screamed.

I hadn't been quite fast enough—the bolt of magic still flew from David's palm, and I heard Blythe cry out from behind me—but I didn't think he'd hurt her all that badly. He'd barely had any time before I was on him, and then all his concentration was on me, flinging more glowing bolts from his hands, the magic hitting the metal of my sword and throwing up sparks.

"David, please," I heard myself say in a voice that didn't sound anything like mine. It was desperate and choked and raspy, and the words seemed to come up from somewhere deep inside me. "Please."

David's hands were working almost as fast as my arms, the two of us stalking each other around the cave. "You'll kill me," he said, and this time there was less of the echo—less of the

Oracle—in his voice, more of just David. "I saw it. I've always seen it."

He threw a particularly strong bolt that had me wincing even as I deflected it, and I was pretty sure I felt something give in my shoulders. I was strong, but not strong enough, not without my powers.

Still, I held my ground. "Not everything you see comes true," I said to him, sweat and tears stinging my eyes. "David, you know that. You said it yourself, that you see"—I broke off as another jolt reverberated off the sword—"what *could* happen. This—" Taking a deep breath, I ignored all the pain in my body and said, "It doesn't have to happen."

He paused. Not for long, just the space of a heartbeat, and I held my breath, praying.

Blythe was behind me, and while I couldn't see her, I could sense her presence and could tell when David suddenly remembered she was there, too. But then something in his face changed, and I glanced back to see that Bee had joined Blythe there, both of them staring at me with wide eyes, Blythe's hands out like she was pleading. "Do it!" she yelled out. "Harper, you have to!"

David lifted his own hand, and there was nothing in his face of the boy I'd loved now. Not one part of him that wasn't Oracle.

I could feel pressure—magic—building, my ears popping with the force of it, and then David looked right at me with those glowing eyes and said one word: "Choose."

It was like everything suddenly slowed down. I felt the weight of the sword in my hand, saw the golden light crackling between

David's fingers, and knew that whatever magic he had there, whatever spell he was about to throw at Bee and Blythe, it was strong enough to kill.

So I chose.

It's harder to drive a sword through someone than you could ever think, and even harder when you love that person. Too hard, almost unbearable, and I felt my own heart shatter as I shoved the blade through his chest.

There was a distant roaring in my ears, and the light faded from David's eyes, his hands dropping limply to his sides as he hit his knees. When he lifted his head, there was still a lot of golden light in his eyes, but not so much that I couldn't see some of the blue beneath it. "Harper," he murmured, and then he slumped to the cave floor, eyes sliding closed.

Everything was still for a moment, and then I felt Bee's hands on my shoulders, holding me close as Blythe stepped forward, falling to her knees beside David.

Blythe knelt on the rock next to David, his blood staining her yellow dress. The sword in my hands felt like it weighed about a million pounds, and I let it drop with a clatter that echoed through the cave. Tears and sweat were running down my face, and I had never been so tired in all my life. Sinking down, I crouched next to Blythe, and my voice was hoarse when I said, "It's over. Is that why you came after us? To make sure I'd do it?"

Blythe's fingers fluttered over David's wound, and she was shaking her head. "No," she said, "I mean. Yes. I came to make sure you'd go through with it, that you'd see it was the only way we could . . ."

Trailing off, she looked at David, her own face nearly as pale as his. "This doesn't feel like we fixed it," she said at last, and all I could do was nod, biting my lip to keep from sobbing.

"I thought it would," she said, and her hand finally touched David's chest, his blood bright against her fingers. "I honestly thought this was the best way."

Keeping my eyes on the crown of her head rather than David's body, I took a deep breath and said, "It was, in the end. It was the only way. You were right, Blythe. I'm not sure there was any spell that could've saved him."

And then I felt Blythe's hand on mine and tried to ignore the heave in my stomach at how warm and sticky her grip felt, her palms still smeared with blood. "I could still try," she said, and I opened my eyes then, blinking at her.

"Blythe—"

"No, I can," she said, one hand still on mine, the other on David's chest. "It isn't too late, I don't think. I can try . . ."

I just shook my head. "He's dead, Blythe."

But Blythe only turned back to David, hand still pressed to his chest. "Just a little bit," she replied, like it was the most normal thing in the world. Like someone *could* be "a little bit dead."

And then she looked back at me. "Do you trust me, Harper?"

Weirdly enough, in spite of everything, I did. Or maybe *because* of everything. Blythe had never lied to us. She had earned at least a little trust.

I nodded, and she reached out to clasp my shoulder, leaving a bloody handprint behind.

Turning back to David, she kept her hands on his chest, murmuring low, but nothing seemed to be happening.

She pressed her hands harder, started speaking again, a little louder this time, and I waited.

But there was nothing. No sound, no breath, no sense in my chest of that pull between me and David, and on the third time, I decided I couldn't just sit there and watch this, couldn't let myself even start to hope that she was right. It felt easier to get up, to walk out of the cave and into the sunlight.

Bee followed behind me, and once we were outside, she looked at me for a second before stepping forward and wrapping me in a hug so tight I swore my bones creaked. She was so much taller than me that my nose was smushed against her collarbone, but I didn't care. For a long while, we just stood there on the path outside the cave, our arms locked around each other.

"We did it," she said, her voice thick. "*You* did it."

It should've felt like a triumph, but all I felt was hollow. I'd kept David from turning any more hapless girls into Paladins, and ensured that he'd never be another Alaric, a dangerous Oracle who could wreak havoc and hurt the people I loved.

But I'd lost him, so what did it matter?

"You don't believe her, do you?" she said to me once we parted, and I could just shake my head. I wanted to believe it, and Blythe had definitely used some powerful magic in the past, but I'd hoped too many times now for miracles or easy fixes, and been disappointed every time. In the end, I'd done what I came here to do, and it was over now.

Over.

Bee and I trudged back down the trail, and I made sure to roll up the sleeve of my T-shirt to hide the bloodstain there. I'd left the sword back in the cave, and I hoped I'd never have to see it again.

We were all the way to the bottom of the mountain when a sort of booming vibration stopped us both in our tracks.

Turning, I looked back up the mountain and saw a flock of birds whirl screeching into the sky, and I waited there, wanting to feel . . . something.

Some sign that that sound had come from a cave tucked deep in the woods where Blythe had worked a miracle. I waited to feel the tug to David that I always felt, like an invisible cord was connecting us.

But there was no feeling, no sense of anything other than loss and exhaustion. I felt the same way I had when I'd plunged that sword into him. He was gone, and I could sense it with every cell. No Oracle, no David.

Nothing.

And after a long while, I turned to Bee and said, "Let's go home."

Chapter 36

THE FIRST DAY of senior year dawned hot and sticky, the way the beginning of every school year started. August in Alabama was a real beast, but there was something nice about it, the way that first blast of air-conditioning hit you when you walked into the school buildings, the way we were all still in summer clothes, the sharp scent of just-cut grass in the air.

This was the year I'd been looking forward to since I'd started school. The year I'd always dreamed that everything would happen for me. Another Homecoming crown, college acceptance letters, cheering at fall football games . . .

But as I made my way through that first day, I couldn't escape the feeling of something missing. And of course, there was something missing. Or rather, someone.

Lord knew I'd spent a lot of time thinking of David lately. Once we'd gotten safely back to Pine Grove, once some of the shock of all that had happened had faded, I'd felt ashamed of how I'd left things in Tennessee. I should've gone back to the cave, shouldn't have let my grief and my fear of seeing him lying there—really, truly dead—keep me from saying good-bye. From seeing him one more time.

But I was determined to put those thoughts out of my head. I had a senior year to ace and a school to run. It was time to turn my attentions back to those responsibilities.

The twins were in the parking lot, as usual, both in the same color—pink today—and while Amanda's hair flowed loose over her shoulders, Abi's had been chopped into a cute bob over the summer.

"I like!" I told her, gesturing to my own hair, and with a little shriek, she ran toward me, Amanda close behind. They both threw their arms around me, locking me in a hug that smelled like Clinique perfume and lavender. To my surprise, I almost teared up.

"Girl, we *missed* you!" Amanda said, and Abi nodded, nearly bumping the top of my head with her chin.

Before I'd left, the twins had been avoiding me, either from the weirdness last spring, or just because they hadn't exactly been high up on my list of priorities, either.

The twins pulled back, watching me with identical hazel eyes, and then Abi frowned a little and said, "You're going to help tutor me in AP Government, right? I have no idea why I signed up for that."

Laughing, I nodded. "You got it."

Leaving the two of them at the courtyard, I walked into the main building, waving at a couple of people—Lucy McCarroll; Bee's ex, Brandon—and made my way toward the lockers.

Ryan and Bee were already waiting for me, and I rolled my eyes at them even as I smiled. "Y'all gonna walk me to class?"

"Yes," Ryan said immediately, and Bee elbowed him in the ribs. "We were hoping not to be so obvious," she said, moving her bag to her other arm, "but . . . okay, what he said."

"You remember the part where I said that I really am okay, right?" I asked both of them, looking up into their faces. "How we had this whole moment when me and Bee got back, there at the Waffle Hut, and y'all were like, 'Are you okay?' and then I confirmed I *was* indeed okay, and we all said the word 'okay' so many times, it stopped sounding like a word? Remember all of that? It was quite a moment."

Ryan reached out and, honest to God, ruffled my hair. "Hey!" I said, laughing a little as I stepped back. "We're not dating anymore, but that doesn't mean you get to treat me like your rapscallion cousin."

"'Rapscallion,'" Bee scoffed, and I gave a shrug, smoothing my hair back into place.

"Boning up on my SAT vocabulary," I said, and she winced.

"Don't say 'boning.'"

All three of us laughed, and for a second, it was like nothing had changed. "I'll meet you dorks for lunch," I told them, "in the courtyard, usual table."

After confirming that Bee and I did have our second-period class together, we headed off: Ryan and Bee to first-period Spanish, while I went in the opposite direction, heading for the headmaster's office. As reigning SGA president, it was my responsibility to meet with any new students we might have this year in twelfth grade. I hadn't heard of anyone, but then it wasn't like I'd been focusing a huge amount on school stuff lately.

There was a flurry of activity around the main office, but that was always the way it was on the first day, and I was already thinking ahead to my own first-period class (AP French—at least half of my schedule was AP classes this year) when the office door opened and someone came hurrying out.

I was looking down as we collided, staring at the person's shoes, a truly heinous pair of houndstooth Chucks, and wasn't sure if my sharp inhale was from who those shoes reminded me of or the force of the collision. "Oh!" I gasped, my bag slipping off my arm.

I glanced down at it, only to find myself almost gasping again when I looked up.

David.

"Ah, God, sorry," he said, reaching for my bag and sliding it back up onto my shoulder. He barely touched me as he did it, his eyes not quite on my face while I stood there, my mouth hanging open, everything in me seeming to somehow go still and speed up all at once. My face felt numb, my hands suddenly freezing, and I had the bizarre idea that maybe I wasn't even at school. Maybe I'd fallen asleep, and—

But then the door opened behind him, and Blythe was standing there in a sensible sweater set and khaki skinny jeans, her dark hair caught up in a chignon at the back of her neck. She looked older than I was used to seeing her, although that weird little glint was still there in her eyes. This time, it looked a lot like triumph.

I realized David was still staring at me, and I made myself look at him.

His sandy hair wasn't sticking up, but then it wasn't fourth period yet. The freckles spreading across his face seemed darker against his slight blush, and his eyes behind his glasses were blue.

Just blue. Not a speck of gold to be seen.

But they were also a little blank as they looked at me. Well, not totally blank. There was some curiosity and, I thought, a little bit of appreciation there, but in that "dude looks at a pretty girl" way.

He didn't know who I was.

My eyes flew past David to Blythe, but before she could say anything, Headmaster Dunn came out in his customary first-day brown suit and green bow tie. "Ah, Harper, excellent. This is David Stark." He clapped David on the shoulder, and David winced a little bit, probably because Headmaster Dunn was wrinkling his shirt.

His lime-green pin-striped shirt.

Blythe might have done something to make him forget everything that had happened, but apparently she hadn't been able to give him new dress sense.

"David, Harper is one of our finest students," Headmaster Dunn continued, like he'd never met David before in his life. Like David hadn't gone to this school since kindergarten, same as me. Again, I glanced to Blythe, and she smirked at me, wiggling her fingers behind Headmaster Dunn's back.

I didn't want to be impressed with that level of mind-control magic, but seeing as how the last time I saw David, he'd been bleeding out on the floor of a cave in Tennessee, I wasn't going to complain.

Headmaster Dunn was still talking—I know he called Blythe David's "sister" at one point—but all I could do was stare at David while trying to pretend I *wasn't* staring at him. He looked so . . . him. Ugly clothes, sharp gaze, hair neater, but probably just seconds away from being a disaster . . .

Headmaster Dunn turned to leave, and as he did, David looked to me, eyebrows raised over the rims of his glasses.

"So I guess you're my tour guide?" he said, and a dimple appeared in his cheek as he smiled.

I found myself smiling back even as I was terrified to even hope it could work out like this.

"Yeah," I said, "let me . . . let me just chat with your, uh, sister for a sec."

I stepped aside, and Blythe moved closer, her back to David, her head lowered so that she could pitch her voice just for my ears.

"I kick so much ass, right?" she asked, smile wide, eyes bright, and despite everything, I laughed. It was shaky and maybe a little unhinged, but it was a laugh.

"How?" I asked, and then suddenly, I knew. "The other spell. The one that freaked Dante out."

She nodded. "Resurrection spell. Terrifying, and nothing I *ever* want to try again, but—"

"It worked," I finished.

"I told you," she said, fiddling with the hem of her sweater. I had no idea how she wasn't sweating to death, but she definitely looked the part of Responsible Older Sister Guardian. "I am *so* badass. Granted, those spells were a lot easier to do on someone who was more or less dead than it would have been a conscious, pissed-off rogue Oracle."

Folding her arms over her chest, Blythe continued. "Although trust me, that was nothing compared to the work it took to get your whole freaking town to forget David had been here before."

For a second, I just blinked at her, afraid I might do something crazy like cry. But instead, I did something even crazier.

I hugged her.

She just stood there as I squeezed her tight, but after a minute, I felt her arms come up tentatively to wrap around me, too, and when we pulled away, she was smiling at me. A real smile. Little and hesitant, but not even the littlest bit unhinged.

"*This* is redemption, right?" she asked. "Like you talked about? I mean, I fixed it. Granted, it's possible he's going to remember eventually, and that's gonna be a real pain in the ass, but—"

I nodded at her, suddenly aware of David watching us curiously. He had to wonder why I was hugging his sister, and we'd probably lingered here too long. So I took a deep breath through my nose and backed up from Blythe.

"Consider yourself redeemed," I told her.

A dimple appeared in her cheek as she gave a quick nod, clearly satisfied, and then her gaze slid to David. "Have a good first day," she told him. "I'll . . . make dinner. Or something."

David shrugged his shoulders, and I found myself wondering

just how that living arrangement was going to work. The idea of Blythe as anyone's guardian was a little scary, but then I reminded myself that David had done a good job on his own after Saylor was gone, so maybe he'd survive having Blythe as a roommate.

I turned back to him now, feeling almost like I should pinch myself. He was so . . . *here*.

He smiled a little at me, then gestured for me to lead the way. I did, rattling off facts about the school, about the town, anything I could think of even as my mind whirled. In the cave, Blythe had said she had a way to fix him so that he wouldn't be an Oracle anymore, but I'd never thought we'd get to start over, clean slate.

I'd spent my whole life with David Stark, pretty much. Hating him, loving him, protecting him, and, eventually, killing him. Starting over as strangers was going to hurt, even as I wanted to do cartwheels down the hall that he was here, that we had made it through this.

I hadn't realized that I was leading him toward the newspaper classroom until we were there in front of it, and I paused, awkwardly playing with the silver ring on my right hand as I gestured to the door. "This is Journalism," I told him, gesturing at the door, and I realized that I was waiting for him to show some sign of recognition. Blythe had said he might remember one day, and while she'd been convinced it would be a "pain in the ass," I thought maybe—just maybe—it would be a good thing.

Ducking his head to look inside the little window set in the door, David raised his eyebrows.

"Cool. What's your school paper like? I love that kind of thing."

My heart felt so full it seemed like there couldn't be any room left in my chest. "It's good," I told him, "although the last editor was kind of a jerk."

He snorted at that, reaching up to push his glasses up his nose. It was the most familiar gesture in the world, and I found myself looking into his eyes. His blue, blue eyes fringed by long lashes. Just regular eyes in a regular face on a regular boy.

"So what do you do around here?" he asked, and I folded my arms, giving a little shrug. "Everything, really," I told him. "Cheerleading, a few committees, SGA president . . ."

That made one corner of his mouth kick up. There had been a time when I would have kissed that spot, just where a little dimple formed. I couldn't do that now, of course.

But it wouldn't always be that way. I believed that with all my heart.

"SGA president, huh?" he asked. "So can I call you Pres?"

It took me a second to reply, but when I did, my smile was so big, it actually hurt my face.

"Yeah. Yeah, you can."

Acknowledgments

I STARTED THE Rebel Belle series in October of 2008, so I've been living with these books for a long time now. And that, of course, means the people in my *life* have been living with *me* living with these books for a long time! So first and foremost, I have to thank John and Will for putting up with me as I wrestled with another trilogy, as I muttered about Paladins and Oracles and acted out fight scenes in the living room. My books can be filled with angst and drama and craziness because my life is full of the happiness and calm you guys provide me, and I'm so thankful for that.

Thanks, too, to "The Mama," for supporting your weird, scribbling kid and having an Azalea Trail Girl dress made for me even if I never *did* get to wear it.

I write books about Ladies Getting It Done, and I'm lucky enough to have a life full of such amazing ladies. Chantel Acevedo, Ash Parsons, Julia Brown, Victoria Schwab, my sweet "C-Lo," y'all are always there with e-mails or texts or lunches out (and drinks, let's be real), and I love you all bunches.

Thank you, too, to everyone at Penguin/Putnam for all you've done for me and these books. Jen Besser, Mia Garcia, Anna Jarzab, Rachel Lodi, Elyse Marshall, and Tara Shanahan, y'all are an amazing group of women to work with, and I am so appreciative! Tiaras for ALL!

I shudder to think what my books would look like without the fierce and guiding hand of Ari Lewin. I feel so lucky to have gotten to make an entire trilogy with you, and am so proud of our "book babies." And thanks, too, to Katherine Perkins for your smart, insightful notes and your dedication to making these books the best they can be!

I've been fortunate enough to get to work with Holly Root on every book I've ever published, and still think that getting her as my agent was my luckiest break.

For all of you who have stuck with me and Harper through all three books, thank you from the bottom of my heart.